**Tim swept his arm in an arc
and gave a slight bow.
"After you, ma'am."**

Dawn shook her head and chuckled. That
pleased him. He was still trying to get over
the shock of finding out she didn't see him as
the kind of man who kept his word. He was
determined to show her his true character,
though he wasn't sure how. Granted, he could
be rather ruthless in business if the situation
called for it, but in his private life he wasn't so
bad, was he? Introspection didn't show any
major flaws that he was aware of. Therefore, he
planned to prove to Dawn what a great guy he
really was.

Why? The surprising question gave him pause.
Why, indeed? He was Dawn's boss, not her
date. Why should he care about her personal
opinion of him as long as she continued to do
her job well?

**DAVIS LANDING:
Nothing is stronger than a family's love**

Books by Valerie Hansen

Love Inspired

The Wedding Arbor #84
The Troublesome Angel #103
The Perfect Couple #119
Second Chances #139
Love One Another #154
Blessings of the Heart #206
Samantha's Gift #217
Everlasting Love #270
The Hamilton Heir #368

Love Inspired Suspense

Her Brother's Keeper #10
The Danger Within #15

VALERIE HANSEN

was thirty when she awoke to the presence of the Lord in her life and turned to Jesus. In the years that followed she worked with young children, both in church and secular environments. She also raised a family of her own and played foster mother to a wide assortment of furred and feathered critters.

Married to her high school sweetheart since age seventeen, she now lives in an old farmhouse she and her husband renovated with their own hands. She loves to hike the wooded hills behind the house and reflect on the marvelous turn her life has taken. Not only is she privileged to reside among the loving, accepting folks in the breathtakingly beautiful Ozark Mountains of Arkansas, she also gets to share her personal faith by telling the stories of her heart for Steeple Hill's Love Inspired line.

Life doesn't get much better than that!

THE
HAMILTON
HEIR

VALERIE HANSEN

Steeple
Hill®

Published by Steeple Hill Books™

To Joe, who loves me unconditionally.
And to John and Karen, who first inspired me to
find a church home. They are all three so dear,
it brings tears to my eyes.
Special thanks and acknowledgment are given to
Valerie Hansen for her contribution to the
DAVIS LANDING miniseries.

STEEPLE HILL BOOKS

Steeple
Hill®

ISBN-13: 978-0-373-87398-2
ISBN-10: 0-373-87398-0

THE HAMILTON HEIR

Copyright © 2006 by Harlequin Books S.A.

www.SteepleHill.com

Printed in U.S.A.

The father of the righteous shall greatly rejoice; and he that begets a wise child shall have joy in him.

—*Proverbs* 23:24

The Hamiltons of Davis Landing

Nora McCarthy – m – Wallace Hamilton

Jeremy*   Timothy   Amy   Christopher (t)   Heather (t)   Melissa

*(son of Nora and Paul Anderson)

> **Legend**
> m = married
> t = twins

1. Heather's story: BUTTERFLY SUMMER by Arlene James   (LI #356, 7/06)
2. Chris's story: BY HER SIDE by Kathryn Springer   (LI #360, 8/06)
3. Amy's story: THE FAMILY MAN by Irene Hannon   (LI #364, 9/06)
4. Tim's story: THE HAMILTON HEIR by Valerie Hansen   (LI #368, 10/06)
5. Melissa's story: PRODIGAL DAUGHTER by Patricia Davids   (LI #372, 11/06)
6. Jeremy's story: CHRISTMAS HOMECOMING by Lenora Worth   (LI #376, 12/06)

Chapter One

Dawn Leroux tensed the moment her boss pushed open the door of his private office and entered hers. She was hard at work, as usual, so no one could question her diligence. Just the same, there was always a niggling feeling of intimidation associated with being in the presence of Timothy Hamilton.

"I left a short list of personnel on my desk," Tim said. "I'll want their files updated and waiting for me when I get back. It shouldn't take you too long."

"Yes, sir, Mr. Hamilton. Anything else?"

"Not that I can think of."

"Fine. I'll take care of it right away."

Dawn smiled inwardly. She wished she had a nickel for every time she'd told her boss that very thing. Being his administrative assistant wasn't a bad assignment as long as she was quick to respond to his orders—and do things his way. The man was predictable, if nothing else. Whatever he wanted done, he wanted it done *yesterday*.

"Will you be out of the office long?" she asked, pen in hand, as he breezed past her desk.

He pushed back his cuff to check his Rolex. "I have a ten o'clock meeting with Ed Bradshaw in the *Dispatch* office downstairs, then lunch with my mother at twelve. If you need me, we'll probably be across the street at Betty's. Mom prefers the Bakeshoppe."

"I can understand why. The food is delicious." Dawn was making notes. "Is that all?"

"For the moment," Tim said. He tapped the breast pocket of his immaculate gray suit. "If I think of anything else, I'll phone you." He paused. "You'll be here?"

"All day," Dawn said pleasantly, knowing exactly what he meant. "I brown-bagged it today." She gestured toward a lower drawer of her desk to reassure him. Knowing Tim Hamilton, he'd chain her to the stupid desk 24-7 if he thought he could get away with it! The man was so focused on business he made a normal workaholic look like a hopeless slacker.

"Right." Tim was already striding away and disappearing through the door as he spoke.

Dawn heard the outer door close and sighed with relief. She stretched, fingers laced together, hands raised over her head. She loved her job, she really did, but ever since his older brother Jeremy had left town in a huff and Tim had moved up in the

Hamilton Media corporate hierarchy, he'd acted as if his every act was of monumental importance. He even drank his morning coffee with deliberateness. The poor man was more of a machine than a human being, although she knew he'd be incensed if he suspected that anyone, especially a member of his staff, felt sorry for him.

Sighing, she breathed a quick prayer for her boss's mental health—and her own—then rose and went into his private office to retrieve the list he'd mentioned.

She paused at the window overlooking the meandering Cumberland River. Fall had already touched this part of Tennessee. The trees along the water were bright and bold, soon to lose their leaves.

Dawn wrapped her arms around herself and gave a little shiver. Her home state of Louisiana might stay hotter in the summer than a bowl of Mama's homemade jambalaya but it made up for it with mild winters. Though she loved Davis Landing and the Nashville area, there were still times when she longed for a cup of rich Café du Monde coffee and one of their famous beignets dusted with powdered sugar. Thankfully that terrible hurricane had spared the French Quarter of New Orleans.

Her stomach growled. Thinking about food was making her hungry far too early in the day. She swung her long blond hair back with a toss of her head, smoothed her skirt and returned to her desk. At five foot three she didn't have a lot of room to store extra pounds and she didn't want to lose control of her eating habits. There weren't many areas of her life over which she had complete control and she wasn't about to relinquish what little she did have.

The heavy, brass doors of the elevator slid open and Tim stepped out on the ground floor. He knew better than to pass through the lobby and engage either Louise or Herman Gordon in casual conversation so he whipped around and ducked into the newspaper office. The elderly Gordons took their jobs as Hamilton Media greeter and guard far too seriously to suit him, and both were terrible gossips. Unless he wanted to listen to their opinions on everything from the weather to their favorite TV shows, he knew it was best to avoid them entirely.

He waved to his sister, Heather, in passing. She absentmindedly returned his greeting with a nod and a smile while toting an armload of paper out the door toward the elevator. Tim figured she was probably headed back up to her *Nashville Living* office on the second floor. He was pleased to see her applying herself. It was never easy to manage staff and he sure didn't want to have to reprimand anyone in his own family. There were times when he secretly envied his father's unwavering sternness. Wallace Hamilton was not a man to trifle with. All six of his children knew that, even Jeremy.

Thoughts of his older brother made Tim's jaw muscles clench. Now that they all knew the truth about Jeremy's parentage it explained a lot. No wonder he'd never had the inherent drive or the business savvy of Wallace's other children. The biggest puzzle was why a perfectionist like Wallace had allowed a laid-back guy like Jeremy to run Hamilton Media at all.

Tim brushed aside his troubling musings and headed straight for the editor's office. Bradshaw's desk was so piled with papers it looked like a copy machine had exploded on it. Tim would have chastised him for his lack of organization if he'd been present.

Frustrated, Tim whirled and accosted the first *Dispatch* employee he came to. "Lyle. Where's Bradshaw? Have you seen him?"

"Sorry. Don't have a clue, boss," the seasoned reporter said. "Maybe Felicity knows where he's at."

Wondering what the man's grades in English class had been, Tim scanned the half-walled cubicles in the newsroom. Heads down, fingers flying on keyboards, everyone was so busy looking busy it was hard to tell who was who.

He finally spotted Felicity Simmons, his brother Chris's girlfriend, returning from the company break room. "Felicity!"

"I was just getting a cup of coffee, Mr. Hamilton," she said quickly as she glanced at her watch. "I was only gone twelve minutes, so technically I'm coming back early."

"I don't care about that," Tim said, annoyed. "I want to know if you've seen Bradshaw."

She glanced over her shoulder. "Ed? I passed him in the hall. He was just leaving. Said something about a sick cat, I think. I suppose he was going home."

"Terrific." Tim scowled. "Okay. Maybe I can catch him in the parking lot. Thanks."

"You're welcome, Mr. Hamilton. Have a good day."

Tim's scowl deepened. *A good day?* A good day was when things flowed smoothly, not when you had unforeseen changes foisted on you. If Bradshaw really had gone home to look after a sick animal instead of keeping their appointment, Tim was going to mention more than his poor office housekeeping. He wasn't about to try to run a publishing empire like Hamilton Media without the complete support of his staff, from the senior editors all the way on down to the likes of Louise and Herman Gordon. Wallace had always understood that and so did Tim. There was no other way to ensure success.

He took an incoming cell phone call with his usual efficiency, waving at the Gordons in passing but not slowing his pace as he left the building. "Oh, hi, Mom. How's Dad this morning?" He knew the answer but felt he had to ask.

"There's been no change," Nora said sadly. "Are you sure you can spare the time to have lunch with me? I know how busy you are and—"

"Nonsense. I always have time for you, you know that." He slid behind the wheel of his silver

BMW, slammed the door and turned the key in the ignition.

"I know, but…"

"Where are you now?"

"At the hospital. Where else?"

"Exactly," Tim said. "You've been spending way too much time there for your own good. You won't do Dad any good if you ruin your health, too."

He slipped the car into Reverse and started to back out of his reserved spot in front of the old brick building they'd renovated to house Hamilton Media. Before he headed for Bradshaw's house he'd cruise the employee parking lot and see if the editor's car was still there. Felicity might have been wrong. There was no sense running all over town if he didn't have to.

Tim had the tiny cell phone pinned between his chin and shoulder. He felt it starting to slip and made a grab for it, leaning to one side in the process. "Oops!" He recovered. "Sorry, Mom. Almost dropped you."

That moment of inattention was all it took to ruin his morning completely. He glanced up, never dreaming he'd see another car so close. The sun was in his eyes, half blinding him. His foot twitched instinctively, only it was poised over the accelerator, not the brake pedal. In the split second it took for him to realize his mistake and switch to the brakes, his bumper had smashed the other car's grille.

Astounded, Tim bit back a colorful comment. That idiotic driver had come out of nowhere! Why didn't people watch where they were going?

"Tim?" his mother said, "are you okay? I thought I heard a crash."

"Fender bender," Tim said. "I'm fine."

"Oh, honey. I'm so glad you're all right. I'll talk to you later, okay? Call me if we're still on for lunch?"

"Sure."

Flipping the phone closed, Tim climbed out of his luxury car, fully expecting to confront the careless driver who had run into him. He shaded his eyes from the glare that had temporarily distorted his perception during the accident. His jaw went slack. There was no adversary to argue with. He'd smashed into an empty parked car! How embarrassing.

He removed his suit jacket as he circled the accident scene and hunkered down to assess the damage. The car he'd hit looked like a clunker but its owner probably valued it just the same. He'd better jot down the license number and drop it off for his administrative assistant to deal with before he left the lot.

Rather than phone from there and possibly have to explain his stupidity in the presence of passing employees, he decided to return to the office and make sure Dawn understood his wish to assume complete responsibility for what had occurred.

He still couldn't fathom how he'd made such a careless mistake but he had. Naturally he'd pay for whatever repairs were necessary. The poor old junk heap he'd hit was probably on its last legs, anyway. Chances were, taking the little dent out of his bumper would cost as much or more than fixing the crumpled fender and grille of the car he'd hit!

Moving the BMW into the nearest available slot, Tim headed for his office. The sooner he got this over with, the sooner he could get his packed schedule back on track.

Dawn was seated at her computer, transferring the requested personnel files to paper, when Tim rushed through the door and startled her. "Did you forget something?"

"Yeah," he grumbled, "My common sense. You won't believe what I just did."

She swiveled her chair to face him, noticing that he was carrying his jacket and looked a lot less *GQ* than usual. "Excuse me?"

"Out there." He nodded in the direction of the parking lot. "I was talking to my mother and I fumbled the phone. By the time I caught it, I'd run into another car." He tossed a scrap of paper onto Dawn's desk. "There's the license number. It wasn't much of a car to start with but it's less of one now. See if you can find out who it belongs to and offer to fix it, will you?"

"Of course." She picked up the paper. Her eyes widened. Her hand began to tremble. "How—how badly is the car damaged?"

"I don't know." He was pacing. "Those things always look worse than they really are. That particular car wasn't in very good shape before I hit it. The owner will probably try to stick me with an exorbitant repair bill but it can't be helped. The fault was all mine."

"Oh, dear." When she looked up at her boss she knew he had no idea whose car he was talking about. Unshed tears misted her vision. She needed that car. Desperately. Not only was it her sole means of transportation, others were depending on her, too.

Tim paused, approached the opposite side of her desk and leaned over it, frowning. "Are you all right?"

"No," she said honestly, "I'm not." Without explanation she grabbed her keys and headed for the door.

"Hey! Where are you going?"

Not taking into consideration that her boss might decide to trail after her, Dawn reached the elevator at a run and smacked the button for the ground floor with the heel of her hand. The heavy brass door was closing as Tim approached and she was too distracted to hold it for him.

She was nearly to the parking lot when her breathless boss finally caught up to her.

He reached for her arm. "Wait a second. What are you doing?"

She wrenched free. "Looking at my car."

"*Your* car?" He had to hustle to keep up with her.

"Yes, my car." Dawn's mouth dropped open as she got her first look at the mangled vehicle. It was worse than she'd imagined. Not only was her grille smashed in, there was greenish fluid in a widening puddle beneath the front end. With a punctured radiator, that car wasn't going anywhere. Not even in an emergency.

"You killed it!" Without taking time to censor her words she spun to confront Tim. "You killed my car!"

"Don't get hysterical," he said calmly. "I told you I'd fix it and I will. Just have it seen to and send me the bill."

"It's not that simple. You have other cars. I don't. I *need* this one."

"Okay, rent one somewhere. That's no problem. I'll pay for it, too."

"Rent another car? I hadn't thought of that."

"You would have, once you settled down. You're just upset right now."

"You can say that again!"

"Look, I told you I was sorry and I meant it. Why don't you call the garage that takes care of our delivery vans and have them tow it to their place for you? Even if they can't fix it they'll undoubtedly know someone who can."

Though she was still trembling, Dawn had to admit he was making sense. "Okay. I'll do it right away. Maybe it isn't as bad as it looks."

"That's right. And even if it is, they can probably give you something you can drive till it's fixed. If not, go ahead and rent yourself some nice wheels, like I said. On me."

"Thanks." She managed a wan smile. "I guess that will solve my problems."

"Of course it will." His jacket hung over his

shoulder on his thumb. He swung it around and put it back on, straightening his tie. "Well, then, if you're satisfied, I'll be on my way."

"How about your Beamer?" Dawn asked belatedly. "Was it badly damaged?"

Tim shook his head and glanced at the slot he'd pulled into after the accident. "Just a scratch and a little dent in the bumper. Nothing serious." One corner of his mouth turned up in a cynical smile. "The only real casualty was your car." His smile spread to include both sides. "Hey. While you're at it, why don't you have the whole thing repainted? Looks like it's pretty rusty in places."

Her left eyebrow arched as she shaded her eyes with one hand and stared up at him, her other hand fisted on her hip. "And charge it to you?"

"Well…sure. Why not? Have to keep the help happy, don't I?"

Dawn immediately rued her rash suggestion. "You don't have to do that, you know. I'm not about to quit over a little dented metal."

Tim's smile widened, his eyes twinkling in the bright autumn sun. Dawn didn't think she'd ever seen him smile that broadly, especially not since his father's illness. There was an appealing charm to his expression that gave her heart a little jolt.

You're just overreacting because you're pumped full of adrenaline, she told herself. *And Mr. Hamilton is just being this friendly because he's at fault. There's nothing more to his smile than that, so simmer down, girl.*

Dawn backed away, giving him plenty of extra room in which to return to his car. "Okay," she said. "I'll go back up to the office and call the garage."

Resuming his usual businesslike demeanor, Tim nodded and approached the Beamer. "Good," he said over his shoulder. "And don't worry. Everything will be fine."

Arms folded, she watched him back out and drive away. When you had as much money as Tim Hamilton and his family did, you could fix just about anything, couldn't you? Anything temporal, that is.

Musing, she pressed her lips into a thin line and jiggled her key ring in one hand as she started for her office. Even the Hamilton wealth might not be enough to save Wallace's life, though she hoped it would. Medical science could be wonderful but it sure was expensive. She was still helping her parents pay the enormous medical bills left after her brother's motorcycle accident. Sadly, in Phillipe's case, the treatment had not been enough to give him back the power to walk again. Some things couldn't be bought, no matter how rich a person was.

Dawn sighed, deep in thought, entered the elevator and pushed the button for the third floor. If she hadn't had her faith to sustain her she didn't know how she'd have coped after her only sibling was so badly injured. The lives of everyone in her family had been changed that day. Putting her college education on hold and getting a job at Hamilton Media to help out with the enormous bills was the least she could do.

She wasn't sorry about that. The only thing that still bothered her was why her prayers for Phil's total healing hadn't been answered.

If she lived a hundred more years she knew she'd never understand that.

Chapter Two

By the time Timothy Hamilton had found his missing editor, chewed him out for leaving the office and returned around eleven, he expected Dawn to have settled the problems of her transportation.

"So, I see your car is gone. Did that all work out like I said?"

"No."

He could tell by her grim expression that plenty was still bothering her so he paused at her desk instead of proceeding to his office. "No?"

"No. They towed the car all right. They just don't have anything they can loan me."

"So, rent a car."

"I tried."

Tim was getting perturbed. "And?"

"There are a couple of big conventions in the Nashville area right now and every car for miles around has either been rented or is reserved. Nobody could help me on such short notice."

"That's ridiculous. Somebody has a car available."

"That's what I thought till I tried to find one."

"You called everybody in the book?"

"Everybody. Even the guys that rent clunkers."

"I didn't expect you to stoop *that* low." The minute the words were out of his mouth he regretted them.

"Oh? Why not? It might be a step up from what I usually drive."

"I didn't mean that the way it sounded," Tim said.

She pulled a face. "I know. I've just had a bad morning. Guess I'm a little cranky."

"How long will the repairs take? Did the garage say?"

"No. They'll get back to me with that, hopefully today, but it won't be in time."

"In time for what?" His brow furrowed. "If you need a ride home I'm sure we can arrange something."

"It's more than that," Dawn said. "I volunteer for meals-on-wheels and it's my turn to deliver."

"Tonight?"

"Yes. Two nights this week."

"Uh-oh."

"My sentiments, exactly."

Tim made a snap decision. "Okay. I'll lend you one of my cars till you get yours back. I'd rather it be the BMW than the Ferrari, if you don't mind."

He was pleased to see a little smile starting. The woman was actually pretty, in a well-scrubbed sort of way. Funny he hadn't noticed that before. He'd always seen her as an efficient adjunct to his office but hadn't really paid much attention to her as an individual until today. That was usually the way he liked to keep his business relationships, but in this instance he could see there was need for a little more personal connection.

"You'd do that? Lend me a car, I mean?"

"Under the circumstances, yes," he said.

Dawn shook her head. "I appreciate your offer but I can't accept."

"Why not?"

"Well, besides the fact that I'd be scared to death I might scratch your expensive car, I can't very well show up driving anything like that."

"Why not?"

Dawn huffed. "Because I'd be embarrassed, for starters. And I'd be worried sick to use it for deliveries. Suppose I spilled gravy or something in it?"

"Embarrassed? Why would you be embarrassed to drive a perfectly good BMW?"

"Because a car like that probably costs more than most of my clients earn in a whole year. Maybe more. I try to make them feel comfortable accepting help, not show them how the other half lives."

"And I'm the other half?"

"Something like that."

"I see."

He mulled over her statement and realized she had a valid point. "Okay."

"Okay what?"

"I'll drive you."

"That wasn't what I meant."

"I know. But I am the one who smashed your car so I figure I owe you."

"You don't have to do this."

"Consider me a fellow volunteer, just helping out in a pinch." Tim couldn't believe she was still hesitating.

"Tell you what," Dawn finally said. "I'll make a few calls, see if maybe Pastor Abernathy or Amy are free to deliver tonight."

"Amy? You mean my sister? Why her?"

"Because she's been doing some of the evening meal distribution, too. I thought you knew?"

"I suppose she may have mentioned it." Tim set his jaw. "Look. I happen to know she has a late meeting scheduled. Forget about arranging for a substitute. I'll drive you. Period. In the meantime, do you want me to throw a little mud on the BMW so it won't look too nice?"

Dawn could tell she was out of options so she capitulated. "I don't think that will be necessary. I'll explain when I hand over the meals."

"I'm almost afraid to ask what you plan to say."

"You can hear it for yourself," she told him with a smile. "I'll want you to come inside with me and meet some of my favorites. They're delightful people. I think you'll be pleasantly surprised."

"No more surprised than I am right now," Tim said. "Why have you never talked about doing volunteer work?"

"I guess it never came up," she answered. "You and I don't have many in-depth conversations."

"Well, maybe we should have," he said. "I'm impressed."

"I didn't tell you about it to make points."

"Still, you did," he said with a smile. "I should be in the office all afternoon, after my lunch with my mother, so let me know when you're ready to go."

The rest of Dawn's day flew past in a blur and 5:00 p.m. arrived before she knew it. Normally, she looked forward to taking the meals to her regulars. This evening, however, she was decidedly uneasy. Not only was she faced with having Tim Hamilton acting as her chauffeur, she'd realized belatedly that he was going to have to drive her home, too. Hamilton Media was located in Davis Landing, in the high-rent district along the Cumberland River, while she lived in Hickory Mills, a place often referred to as the "wrong side of the tracks." She didn't relish having her hypercritical boss see her modest apartment, even from the outside.

She considered phoning for a taxi, then changed her mind for fear of offending him. The door to Tim's office stood ajar and she could hear him talking on the phone, so she waited till he'd ended his conversation before rapping on the door and easing it open a bit farther.

"Mr. Hamilton?"

"Yes?"

He had removed his jacket, loosened his pale

blue silk tie and rolled up his shirtsleeves, yet his wavy dark hair was perfectly combed and he still looked like a glossy ad for Armani suits or expensive Italian loafers.

Dawn hesitated, then plunged ahead. "All that correspondence you wanted is stacked on my desk, waiting for your signature."

"Good. Thanks."

"I—uh—I thought I'd go home now."

"Is it that late already?"

"I'm afraid so."

"Then we'd better get going." He stood. "Where do you live?"

"Hickory Mills. On Third Street."

"Then let's go. Can't keep hungry folks waiting for their dinner."

"I still feel bad about this. I wouldn't agree to it except—"

"Except I murdered your car. Have you heard anything about its repair or am I going to have to pay for its funeral, instead?"

"Repair. Definitely repair," Dawn said, smiling. "The garage called. They promised a price break and I told them to go ahead. I hope that was okay."

"Fine. Very efficient, as usual." He slung his jacket over one shoulder, then joined her at the door. "I was going to do a bit more work before I called it a day but I guess I can come in early tomorrow. Let's go."

Having to take two steps for each of his long strides, she was nearly running by the time they got to the elevator. He reached out and held the door for her to pass.

"Thanks," she said. "I'm glad you're not in a hurry. I'd probably have to wear track shoes to keep up with you if you were."

"You were moving pretty fast this morning," Tim countered. "I had to run down the stairs to catch you."

"Good thing you have such long legs then, huh?" Dawn saw him eye her much shorter stature and discerned a touch of wry humor in his expression. "My legs are not too short," she insisted. "They reach all the way to the ground, don't they?"

Tim chuckled. "That, they do."

Suddenly, Dawn wished she'd kept her mouth shut instead of calling attention to herself. She wasn't ashamed of her lithe figure or the feminine clothing she favored, she just hadn't meant for her otherwise reserved boss to take special notice. There had been times, ever since she'd started working for him, that she'd secretly wished he'd at least acknowledge her as a living, breathing human being. Now that he had, however, she wasn't so sure she liked it, especially since they were cooped up in a cramped elevator. Alone.

Don't be silly, her sensible side argued. *There's nothing wrong with taking an innocent elevator ride with a man, no matter how handsome and dashing he happens to be.* And there was certainly nothing wrong with Tim Hamilton's manners. He was every bit the perfect Southern gentleman he'd always been.

Particularly in regard to other women, she added contritely. Until today, his suave graciousness had seemed reserved for women he saw socially. Now that Dawn was the recipient of the Hamilton charm, she wasn't sure how she ought to react. One thing was certain, however. This was going to be a *very* long evening.

If she could have been positive the whole unfolding sequence of events was God's idea, maybe meant to show Tim how to appreciate the simple things in life more, she'd have been happier with the situation. Then again, who was she to question her Heavenly Father?

The same silly person I've always been, she answered honestly. Some things were just beyond human comprehension and the only times she got herself into real trouble were when she tried to second-guess the Lord and help Him out.

That ridiculous thought made her smile. As if God wasn't capable of doing anything He wanted whether she cooperated or not!

When they reached the ground floor, Herman Gordon hailed them. "Night, Mr. Tim, Miss Dawn." He bent to retrieve a picnic basket from beneath the counter that he and his wife, Louise, considered their private bailiwick. "Here's the stuff you ordered from Betty's, sir. It was just delivered a few minutes ago. Miss Justine brought it over."

Tim took the basket from him. "Thanks, Herman. Have a good evening."

The old man waved a clipboard. "Gotta sign out. Them's the rules."

"Do it for us," Tim called back, hurrying Dawn toward the door. "You know who we are."

Dawn snickered quietly. "He's a stickler, isn't he?"

"Wouldn't have it any other way," Tim said. "I just figured we'd better make tracks or he'd start telling us one of his long stories and you'd never get your meals delivered." He led the way to his car. "Speaking of which, I thought we might be hungry, too, so I ordered a little dinner to go."

"That's what's in the basket?"

"Uh-huh." He opened the passenger door and held it for her. "I knew it wouldn't be right to eat anything meant for delivery to your customers, so I planned ahead and ordered this when I had lunch at Betty's today. I hope you don't mind."

"No. Not at all." He handed her the basket, closed her door and laid his suit coat neatly across the backseat before finally getting behind the wheel.

Unsure of what he wanted her to do with the food, Dawn merely sat there on the smooth leather seat and held the basket on her lap.

"Well, aren't you hungry?" Tim asked.

"Sure, but…you don't intend for us to eat in the car, do you?"

"Why not?"

"Because. What if we spill something?"

"Are you a messy eater?" There was evident humor in his tone.

"Not usually." She had to smile. "However, when I'm trying to keep from making a mess, it's much harder not to. Murphy's law, I guess."

"Then it's a good thing I didn't order spaghetti," Tim said, laughing softly. "There are supposed to be three kinds of sandwiches in there, a couple of pickles and some cold bottles of sparkling water with lemon. Anything else was Betty's idea."

"*Three* kinds of sandwiches?" Dawn lifted the lid and peeked into the basket. "You must be really hungry."

"I wasn't sure what you liked and I wanted to cover all the bases, that's all. We can eat what we want and toss the rest in the garbage."

"Not on your life! Where I come from we don't waste food."

Tim started the car and pulled out onto Main Street. "Where *do* you come from? I didn't notice that part of your personnel file when I reviewed it for your promotion."

It struck Dawn as odd that anyone would choose to read a file for background information rather than talk to the person involved. But that was typical Tim Hamilton, wasn't it? Typical, but sad.

"My family's from Louisiana, down by New Orleans." She decided to elaborate rather than have him think she was ashamed of her roots, which she wasn't. "Dad worked on the docks. Mom used to clean houses to help out."

"Are you from a big family like mine?"

"No. There are just two of us. My brother, Phillipe, and me."

"I see. So, what brought you to Tennessee?"

"College. I got a wonderful scholarship to Central Tennessee University."

"Really? That's where my sister Melissa used to go to school."

Dawn nodded. "I never could have afforded CTU if it hadn't been for the scholarship. I was going to become an English teacher."

"But you didn't finish? Why not?"

"Phil, mostly. He had a terrible accident that left him paralyzed. Mom stays home now to take care of him and I do all I can to help them out. The medical bills were unbelievable. Still are. I wouldn't be sitting here talking to you if it hadn't been for all that. It's why I needed a full-time job."

"You're going to go back to school, aren't you?" He sounded genuinely concerned.

"Maybe. Probably. I haven't decided."

"College is vital," Tim said. "We were all upset when Melissa dropped out and took off."

"She's the baby of the family, isn't she?"

"Yes. In more ways than her age." He changed the subject with a nod toward the basket. "Aren't you going to eat something?"

"I guess I should, since you went to all this trouble. What would you like?"

"Considering the morning I had, I think I'd better keep both hands on the wheel, don't you? Go ahead without me. I can grab a bite while you're getting your meals ready or whatever it is you need to do."

"Okay." Dawn lifted the hinged lid of the basket, took out the sandwich on top and bit into it. "Umm. Tuna. Delicious."

She chewed and swallowed, then said, "First, I have a few things I need to do at my apartment. You can eat while I'm changing into something more comfortable." Her cheeks burned the moment she realized the possible salacious interpretation of her innocent remark. "I meant, you can eat while you wait for me in the car."

"Of course."

A sidelong glance at her companion revealed a smile he was trying to subdue. Tim was laughing at her. Oh, not out loud because he was too polite, but he was laughing, all the same. She'd have to choose her words a lot more carefully in the future. Some English major she'd turned out to be! A few minutes alone with Timothy Hamilton and her normally quick wit had fled like a dry leaf in a Tennessee tornado. Although he'd earned the behind-the-scenes nickname, Typhoon Tim, because of his habit of approaching work with the speed of a whirlwind, this was one more reason the name fit. He'd certainly blown her away with his cordiality and innate charisma.

Dawn sighed in self-disgust and concentrated on finishing the first half of her sandwich. As she'd decided earlier, this was going to be a very, very long evening.

* * *

They'd crossed the Cumberland via Mill Road and were approaching the downtown area of Hickory Mills when Tim broke into her contemplation with a question. "Are we getting close?"

"Yes. My apartment is on Third, like I said, near the corner of Market." She screwed the cap back on her bottle of water, then pointed. "You can turn here."

Blotting her mouth with a paper napkin she placed the picnic basket on the seat between them. "This is it. Park anywhere along the street. I won't be long."

"Take your time," Tim said pleasantly. "I'll be right here, relaxing and enjoying my supper."

He swung in parallel to the cracked curb, shut off the engine and got out to open the car door for her. By the time he'd circled the car, however, Dawn had already let herself out.

He stopped short, slipped his hands into his pockets and struck a nonchalant pose while he watched her disappear into the three-story brick building.

The woman was independent, that was for sure. Spunky. And she had the uncanny ability to make him laugh, something he did far too infrequently, especially lately.

She also had a depth of character he'd missed seeing until now. Although he disagreed with her decision to quit school, he understood why a person would do so in order to help his or her family.

If he and Dawn Leroux had nothing else in

common they had that—a deep need to support and maintain the bonds of kinship. He certainly couldn't fault her for that.

Dawn climbed the three flights of stairs and unlocked the door to her apartment. "Beau? I'm home. Where are you?"

The thump of the enormous brindle dog's tail against the hardwood flooring echoed in the otherwise silent room. Dawn smiled as he rose, stretched and lumbered over to greet her. She was able to pat his broad head without reaching or bending. Phil had been fond of saying that a mastiff was a lazy man's dog and Dawn had to agree. Not only was Beauregard so laid-back he rarely moved faster than a walk, he also remained quiet and calm in the face of almost anything, making him ideal for an apartment.

She snickered to herself as she led the dog down the back stairs and released him into the small yard that backed up to an overgrown drainage ditch. Why should Beau get excited? There wasn't much he couldn't handle if he had to. His mere size generally precluded the necessity to act. No human or animal in its right mind would challenge a dog with a muscled body the size of a pony, jaws as strong as an alligator's and a tongue as broad as her palm.

Finished sniffing the grass and weeds, Beau returned to her as if they'd been together all his life. Dawn was thankful she'd been able to adopt him as a favor to her brother after Phil's crippling accident. Their agreement had been for her to temporarily care for the big dog but, although it remained unsaid, Dawn and Phil both knew Beau would never go back to Louisiana.

She didn't bother to leash him as they climbed the stairs together. Beau loved three things. Human companionship, food and naps, pretty much in that order. Since she was his best buddy and they were headed in the direction of his food dish, there was no chance Beau would stray.

As a matter of fact, he beat her to the door, pushed past her legs, headed straight for his dish and sat patiently waiting for his dinner.

Kibble rattled into the bowl as she poured from the bag of dog food before she gave him fresh drinking water.

He was crunching happily as she straightened and patted him on his broad, mottled-brown back. "Okay, baby, enjoy. I'll be back as soon as I can. I promise. You be good while I'm gone, okay?"

His tail wagged faster in reply, though his nose remained buried in the food.

She laughed. "Good. Stay right there so you don't accidentally get me dirty. I'm going to go change. I have *not* been having a very good day."

The foolishness of conversing with a dog struck Dawn funny. Old Beau might not be a very good conversationalist but he sure was easy to talk to, wasn't he?

It was just as well Beau wasn't able to give sage advice, she reasoned as she proceeded to don jeans and a blue short-sleeved sweater and run a brush through her hair. If she could think of any way to get out of spending the evening driving around with her persnickety boss, she'd send him packing in a heartbeat.

Chapter Three

❧

Northside Community Church was well known not only because of its place in the history of Hickory Mills and Davis Landing, but also because it had a reputation for running exemplary outreach programs. The community kitchen and its preparation of meals-on-wheels was one such endeavor. The youth program was another.

Behind the white-painted brick facade and wide, columned portico of the original, more traditional church sat a more modern complex of two-story buildings in which that kind of humanitarian work was carried on daily.

Tim had known about the programs before he'd become Dawn's temporary chauffeur but seeing one of them in operation gave him further appreciation of all the effort that went into managing such important projects.

It also showed him how well-respected his administrative assistant was in the community. Although she was a Tennessee transplant, she'd apparently been totally accepted by everyone at Northside, natives included.

Watching her greet the other kitchen volunteers so fondly gave him pause. Clearly, there were places where she was more fully accepted than he was, even though he and his family were an integral part of the entire area's history and current prosperity.

Dawn stood aside, tugged the hem of her short-sleeved sweater over her jeans to smooth it and motioned him to come on into the kitchen. "Ladies, you know Mr. Hamilton? I had car trouble tonight and he was kind enough to offer to drive me on my rounds. Wasn't that nice of him?"

Amid a tittering chorus of welcome, Tim strode forward as if arriving at a board meeting and offered his most amiable smile. "A pleasure to meet you all," he said. "Please, call me Tim."

Shaking hands with those who weren't too deep in kitchen cleanup to offer, he saw Dawn standing back, hesitating. His smile widened. "Yes, you, too, Ms. Leroux. I'm sure it won't destroy office protocol if we're more informal tonight. It'll help your clients relax, especially since they probably haven't met me before, don't you think?"

"I suppose so." She swallowed hard. "Um, Tim."

Tim couldn't help being amused by her obvious nervousness. The woman was practically quaking. What was the matter with her? Did she think he was going to say or do something inappropriate? He'd been to Northside often enough in the past to be familiar with Pastor Abernathy and a few of the regular parishoners, especially the ones he played golf with, so what in the world could be bothering Dawn? She'd seemed just fine when she'd arrived and begun greeting the other workers like long-lost sisters. Now, however, she seemed jittery, as if she couldn't wait to get out of there.

She found her voice moments later and pointed. "Those insulated boxes on the end of the counter are ours. The dinners go inside. If you'll help me carry them to the car we can be on our way."

"Sure." He bestowed amiable smiles all around, said, "If you ladies will excuse us," and joined Dawn. In the background he imagined he heard audible sighs. Those poor women must be exhausted. He wondered if they worked there the whole day.

Following Dawn to the car with the stack of padded boxes he asked about it. "How long do those volunteers work? Is it an all-day shift?"

"We break it down into two, usually," Dawn said. "The earlier shift is much larger. They do the majority of the cooking every Monday, Wednesday and Friday morning. A different bunch puts together the evening meals and cleans the kitchen."

She paused at the rear of his car while he opened the trunk. "Most meals are delivered earlier, between noon and two or three o'clock. That's why there aren't other drivers picking up now. And that's why it was so hard to find someone to take my place. We only have a few regulars who like their food at suppertime and I'm able to handle all the ones in town. I work Monday and Wednesday nights. Amy drives the country route on Fridays."

"I see." He carefully arranged the boxes in the trunk before closing it and starting for the passenger door. Dawn was already there, had it open and was climbing in. Acting like the gentleman his mother had raised wasn't easy where Dawn Leroux was concerned, was it? It didn't matter to Tim whether or not their outing was for pleasure. He didn't have to be dating the lady to want to treat her with propriety.

"I would have gotten that door for you," Tim said, sliding behind the wheel.

"It's not necessary. I'm perfectly capable of taking care of myself."

He gave her a lopsided smile. "I don't doubt that for a second. What I meant was, it's a simple courtesy. One I'm used to offering."

"I'm sorry," she said quietly. "I didn't think of it quite that way."

Tim thought he detected an odd tinge of emotion in her tone as she turned to stare out the side window. He wondered if he'd embarrassed her. He certainly hadn't meant to. He never had understood women, even though he'd grown up in a household with a mother and three sisters. Amy and Heather had never seemed to mind being treated with respect. Melissa? Well, that was another story. Melissa was a special case. She seemed to struggle with personal issues that didn't faze the others.

"Who's our first customer?" Tim asked, taking care to keep his tone light and friendly.

"Stuart Meyers," Dawn said. "He lives alone in one of those shotgun houses all in a row down by the river. It's not far. Go back the way we came and I'll tell you when to turn."

"Right. I haven't heard anybody mention shotgun houses in years. Aren't those the ones that are supposedly so small you can fire a shotgun in the front door and the shot will travel out the back door before the pattern spreads enough to hit anything?"

"I see you know something about history. Stuart will love you. How smart are you about The War?"

"Smart enough to know exactly what you mean and to not call it the *Civil* War unless I'm talking to a Yankee," Tim said with a grin. "I was in school before I'd heard the conflict called anything but The War Between the States."

"It was the same in Louisiana," Dawn said. "Or The War for Southern Independence. That was always my favorite name for it."

"That figures, since you're so independent yourself. I know Tennessee provided troops to both the North and the South. Which does your Mr. Meyers favor?"

"He's not fussy. He loves to argue both sides." Dawn pointed. "Take that narrow road over there. Stuart's is the second house on the right. The one that needs painting."

Tim refrained from saying that he thought all the houses in sight were in serious need of maintenance, most of them too far gone to be saved by a simple coat of paint. He parked as instructed, then released the trunk latch from the driver's seat before getting out.

He was standing at the rear of the car, trying to decide which meal package was which—or if there was any difference—when he noticed that Dawn had not yet joined him. Leaning to one side he peered around the raised trunk lid and saw her sitting primly right where he'd left her.

Was she waiting for him to open her door? Surely not. Not after all her insistence that she could do things herself. Maybe the latch was stuck or something. He was beside the passenger door in three strides, jerked it open without undue effort and stepped back.

Her face glowed and her blue eyes sparkled as she tilted her head to gaze up at him.

Tim's jaw dropped when she batted her long, beautiful lashes, and said in an exaggerated Southern accent, "Why thank you, kind sir. Bless your heart. I'm truly obliged for your gentlemanly behavior."

Dawn didn't know what had come over her all of a sudden. She was brave and had a good sense of humor but she wasn't normally foolhardy. Teasing Tim Hamilton like that, when he was trying so hard to be nice, seemed too over-the-top even for a laid-back Louisianan with Cajun roots.

The fact that he'd recovered from the initial

shock and looked as if he was struggling to keep from laughing helped salve her conscience. She swung her jeans-clad legs out of the car and quickly stood to smooth the hem of her sweater over her hips. "Sorry about that. I couldn't resist."

Tim chuckled and shook his head. "I guess I deserved it for insisting we observe antiquated customs."

"No, you didn't. There's nothing wrong with a few old traditions. As a matter of fact, most of the folks we'll be seeing tonight prefer classic Southern manners. And if that's what suits them, it suits me, too."

"So, you're something of a chameleon, is that it?"

Separating the Styrofoam box containing Stuart's meal from the others, she turned and headed toward his front porch. "I see myself as adaptable, not artificial. If I notice that something I say or do makes someone else uncomfortable, I try to avoid making the same mistake again."

"Point taken," Tim said, falling in step beside her. "From now on, I promise I won't insist on treating you like a fragile Southern belle."

"And I promise I won't chew you out if you forget and try to open a door for me," Dawn countered.

"That's big of you."

If Tim hadn't been grinning so widely that the corners of his eyes crinkled, she might have worried more that he was actually offended. It was hard to tell for sure. He apparently had a sense of humor that let him enjoy a good joke without getting too carried away.

Unlike my dad, she added, remembering fondly how her father's deep laugh had filled the house till the windows almost shook with it. She was used to boisterous men like him: men who loved life, wore their feelings on their sleeves and were equally at home yelling encouragement from the stands at a softball game or shouting a reverent "Hallelujah" from a church pew.

No wonder her reactions to Tim Hamilton were rather odd, she mused. He was so unlike anyone she'd ever been close to she was half awed, half flabbergasted. It was a wonder their working relationship was so effective, although it seemed to satisfy Tim.

Then again, Dawn reminded herself, at the office she kept her focus on pleasing him and doing everything precisely his way. What was not to like?

She climbed Stuart Meyers's wooden steps, crossed the porch in two strides and knocked. From inside the tiny house she heard, "Hold your horses. I'm comin', I'm comin'," accompanied by the steady thump of the rubber tip of the old man's cane.

Smile in place, Dawn waited patiently. When the door swung open she greeted the white-haired octogenarian and explained why she'd brought a companion. "Evening, Mr. Meyers. Sorry I'm a few minutes late. This is Mr. Hamilton. My car is in the shop and he was kind enough to drive me."

"Well, come on in, come on in," Stuart said brightly. "It's not often I have company like this. "Y'all can stay, can't you?" He paused to wink up at Tim. "The mister here and I can have a little sip of something smooth from Kentucky, if you know what I mean."

"Sorry, but no thanks," Tim said. "I'm driving, remember?"

"Pity. I been savin' that bottle for a special occasion." He hobbled into the main portion of the house that served as both living room and kitchenette.

Dawn followed and placed Stuart's dinner on a TV tray for him. She eyed the large oval table that he used for everything but eating. It was arrayed with toy soldiers, plastic artillery, rail fences made of twigs, and strategically placed piles of sand and dirt. "I see nobody's won yet," she said. "How's the war going?"

Stuart snorted as he shuffled past the overstuffed chair where he usually took his meals and proceeded to the table to peer at his handiwork over the upper rim of his glasses. "Not good," he said. "General John Bell Hood's Army of the Tennessee just let Schofield's troops sneak through Spring Hill during the night and Hood's about to get his you-know-what kicked at Franklin. Lost six Confederate generals there, you know."

Tim nodded. "Go on."

"Hood would be a fool to press on to Nashville and attack General Thomas after that, but that's exactly what he's gonna do. Guess he thought he could lead Sherman on a wild-goose chase and keep him out of Savannah. Might of worked, too, if he'd been able to move fast enough and recruit more men on the march."

Tim circled the table, assessing the battlements and curving strips of blue paper that evidently represented the wanderings of a river. "Is this the Cumberland where it runs through Nashville? Looks like the fortifications on Overton's Hill." It was a wild guess but Tim was rewarded with a gleeful shout from the old man.

"It is! And over here's Shy's Hill." A gnarled finger pointed. "The second Union attack begins here, on Hood's right flank. It fails till Major General Smith's men take Shy's Hill and show 'em how it's done."

"Where's Nathan Bedford Forrest?"

"South. In Spring Hill," Stuart said. "I'm a tad short of cavalry horses or you could tell by lookin'."

"I'm sure I could," Tim said. "You've done a marvelous job setting this up."

"Thanks, son. It's a pleasure to talk to somebody who knows his history like you do. Most kids these days couldn't care less."

Tim's gaze darted to Dawn's face in time to see her hide a snicker behind her hand. He didn't really mind hearing the elderly gentleman refer to him as a kid at thirty-three. Given their age differences, he supposed Stuart thought of anyone under sixty as still wet behind the ears.

"You should eat now, Mr. Meyers," Dawn said. "Your supper's getting cold."

"Eat? How can I eat when Nashville's under siege?" He circled the table and grabbed Tim's forearm. "Come on. You can be Nathan Bedford Forrest, since you mentioned him. You bring your troops north from Franklin and lead a surprise attack on Thomas's rear!"

Tim laughed. "Sorry. I'm afraid I have another assignment tonight, sir."

The old man's shoulders sagged. "Oh, right. You're on mess duty. I forgot."

"Maybe another time," Tim told him gently. "I'd like to hear more. The history of this area has always fascinated me. My great-great-grandfather, Jeremiah Hamilton, settled here in the nineteen twenties."

Stuart's eyes squinted behind his glasses. "Hamilton, you say? Thought I recognized that name when you came in. Well, well, well. I knew old Jeremiah's boy, Fred. We joined the Marines when we was barely old enough to shave. Fine man, rest his soul. You come from good stock, boy."

Tim smiled. "Thank you, sir." He was edging toward the door where Dawn waited. "Looks like I'd better go before everybody else's food gets cold."

He hesitated when Stuart hobbled closer, extended his right hand and said, "I'm proud you came. It's been a pleasure, son."

"The pleasure is all mine," Tim replied sincerely, shaking hands.

"By Wednesday night I can have all the fortifications slicked up and we can have a real set-to."

Tim glanced at Dawn. Her jaw looked a little slack and her blue eyes were wider than he'd ever seen them before. He made a snap decision. "If it happens that I'm not needed to deliver meals then, I'll still drop by again some time. I promise."

Stuart's shoulders slumped. He sounded down in the dumps when he said, "You do that, son. You do that."

Dawn walked as far as the car before she whirled and confronted Tim. "You shouldn't have promised him."

"Why not?"

"Because he'll be terribly disappointed when you don't show up."

"Who says I won't show up?"

"I do." Her hands fisted on her hips. "I know your work schedule, remember? You hardly have time to breathe, let alone visit lonely old men and spend hours rehashing the Civil War."

"Then I'll make time," Tim said firmly. "I don't know where you got such a low opinion of me but it's wrong. I never make a promise I don't intend to keep. I said I'd see Stuart Meyers again and I will."

Dawn just stared. "You will? You really will?"

"Yes. I will." He circled the car and opened the driver's door. "Now, are you coming? Or are you going to stand there arguing and let the rest of this food get colder than it already is?"

* * *

Several other stops were uneventful and the deliveries went quickly. Ada Smith was next to the last on the evening circuit.

As Tim parked in front of her run-down antebellum home, Dawn filled him in. "Miss Ada is a dear. She absolutely dotes on her grandchildren, so be sure to mention how attractive they are when she shows you their photos."

"How do you know she will?"

Dawn laughed lightly. "Oh, she will. She always does. And if any of them have been to see her recently, we'll be treated to a minute-by-minute replay of their visit."

"Okay." Tim opened the trunk, took out another dinner and passed it to Dawn. He swept his arm in an arc and gave a slight bow. "After you, ma'am."

She was shaking her head and chuckling. That pleased him. He was still trying to get over the shock of finding out she didn't see him as the kind of man who kept his word. He was determined to show her his true character, though he wasn't sure how. Granted, he could be rather ruthless in business if the situation called for it, but in his private life he wasn't so bad, was he? Introspection didn't show any major flaws that he was aware of. Therefore, he planned to charm the socks off the little old lady he was about to meet and prove to Dawn what a great guy he really was.

Why? The surprising question gave him pause. *Why, indeed?* He was Dawn's boss, not her date.

Why should he care about her personal opinion of him as long as she continued to do her job well? Dropping back a few paces he frowned with introspection as he watched her make her way onto the sagging wooden porch.

The front door flew open before Dawn could knock. A pixieish old woman with a wide grin and a head full of tight white curls reached for Dawn's arm and practically dragged her inside.

"There you are, girl! I was gettin' worried."

"Sorry we're a little late, Miss Ada. We got delayed when Stuart Meyers started talking about The War. You know how that goes."

Ada chortled. "That, I do. My Sidney was a jewel, Lord bless him, but when he got to talkin' about huntin' or fishin' he was as single-minded as one of his old hound dogs trailin' a possum." Blue eyes twinkling, she giggled behind her hand like a youngster. "'Cept, as I recall, Sid didn't bay at the moon near as much as them dogs did."

Dawn laughed with her, then turned back to the doorway where Tim waited politely. "I have someone with me tonight, Miss Ada. I'd like you to meet Tim Ham—"

"Land sakes!" the old woman shouted, cutting off the introduction. "Why didn't you tell me you were bringin' a friend? Hoo-whee, he's a big 'un." She lowered her voice to continue but it was still loud enough to have been heard all the way to the curb. "Mighty good-looking, too. Reminds me of a fella I dated years ago. That boy sure could kiss."

"Miss Ada!" Dawn's voice was raised, too.

"Oh, posh. Don't be such a prude, girl."

"Mr. Hamilton and I are not romantically involved," Dawn insisted. "I had car trouble and he was kind enough to drive me on my rounds tonight."

Ada eyed Tim. "That right?"

He nodded. "Yes, ma'am."

Her pale brows arched. "Well, well. And I suppose you're gonna tell me you ain't noticed what a pretty little thing our Dawn is. There's men'd fight to marry her for that long blond hair, alone."

Cheeks reddening, Tim looked as though he was trying his best to keep a straight face. The corners of his mouth twitched. His dark eyes shone. "Yes, ma'am."

Ada was just getting warmed up. She held out her arms toward Dawn as if hawking a priceless treasure. "Look at that girl. She's pretty as a speckled pup. Smart, too. Went to college. Did you know that?"

"Yes, ma'am, I did."

Dawn broke in. "I work for Mr. Hamilton, Miss Ada. I'm his administrative assistant."

"His what?"

"Secretary," Dawn said flatly. Determined to change the subject she asked, "So, how are all your grandchildren?"

"Oh, they're wonderful. Sissy's about to graduate and Bubba's got his first girlfriend. The little ones are cute as ever."

Dawn was relieved to see Ada bustle over to an end table and produce a packet of snapshots which she proceeded to display for Tim, one at a time, along with a running commentary.

He glanced at Dawn over the elderly woman's mop of poodlelike curls. There was a plea for rescue in his gaze.

"We really should be going," Dawn said. "We have one more stop."

Ada looked up. "I'm not the last one?"

"Not anymore. Remember? We added that nice young family, Jordan and Allison Martin."

"Right. The folks with the baby. I forgot. How's the daddy doin'? Think he'll be able to go back to work soon?"

"We hope so," Dawn said. "Since he's a carpenter, I'm not sure. It's not like he can sit behind a desk all day the way I do."

"Pity," Ada said. She slipped the wad of photos back into the envelope. "Well, at least have some of my homemade cookies before you go. I baked extra for when the grandkids come by."

Dawn gave Tim a look that was more warning than anything else as she said, "No, no. You should save them for the children."

"Nonsense. There's plenty. You two just stay put for a second and I'll get you a taste. I can always spare a few." She was leaving the room. "Be right back!"

Tim closed the distance between Dawn and himself before he asked softly, "Why not take a cookie? What would it hurt?"

"Depends," Dawn said with a lopsided grin. "If she remembered to put the sugar in this time, it won't hurt a bit. If she got it mixed up with the salt like she did the last time, that's another story."

Ada returned before Tim could comment. She held out a plastic bag containing four puffy discs of dough that resembled lumpy oatmeal. "I packed 'em up so you could take 'em along."

"Thank you, Miss Ada," Tim said, graciously accepting the gift. "We'll enjoy them while we drive. I'm pleased to have met you."

The elderly woman eyed Dawn. "He's got manners, too, bless his heart."

"That, he does." Dawn was already on her way to the door. "Good night, Miss Ada."

"Night, children," Ada said. "Y'all be good, y'hear." She tittered. "But not *too* good. Life's too short to pass up the chances the Good Lord gives us. Take it from me. If I had it all to do over again…"

Dawn had reached the door, pushed it open and flung herself through. Tim was following too slowly to suit her so she grabbed his shirtsleeve and tugged him along, not letting go till they were at the car.

"I take it she's a widow," Tim said.

"Yes. Has been for ages. If anyone should be out looking for companionship, it's Ada Smith."

Tim chuckled. "Something tells me it would take a very special man to satisfy her. Someone hard of hearing, maybe?"

That made Dawn laugh. "And tolerant. And definitely someone who loves her grandchildren, which is a pretty tall order." She climbed into the car unaided and was fastening her seat belt when Tim slid into the driver's seat.

"She was right about one thing." His hands were on the wheel, his eyes staring straight ahead.

"Oh?"

"Yeah," Tim said quietly. "You really do have pretty hair."

Chapter Four

After they'd completed the meals-on-wheels deliveries and dropped the carrying boxes back at the church, Dawn expected Tim to merely let her off at her apartment and be on his way. However, when he parked, he got out.

She looped the strap of her purse over one shoulder and hesitated on the sidewalk. "Thanks for the ride."

"No problem. I actually enjoyed myself. Some of those people are fascinating."

"Told you so." He was still not making any move to get back into his car and she wasn't sure what to do about it. "Well, good night."

He quickly circled the BMW and joined her. "I'll walk you up."

"That's not necessary."

Tim was firm. "I think it is."

"Well, I don't. I come home every night by myself and go in without an escort."

"Tonight, you have one."

"I don't need one."

"Humor me. I'll feel safer knowing I took you all the way to your door."

"Are you implying that my neighborhood isn't safe at night because I don't live in a gated complex like you do?"

"I didn't say that."

"No, but you implied it."

Tim stared at her, his expression unyielding. "Look. I don't care where you live or what your neighbors are like. You heard what happened to Felicity Simmons. My brother Chris had to be assigned as her bodyguard."

"That was a stalker, not a random crime. Felicity told me all about it."

Tim folded his arms across his chest, struck a nonchalant pose and began to smile. Dawn could tell by the smug look on his face that he wasn't going to back down.

"You're going to stand there all night if I don't let you walk me up, aren't you?" she asked.

"Sure am. I can hold out as long as you can."

"Probably longer," she muttered, pouting. "Okay. You can escort me to my door if it'll make you happy. But that's as far as you go. You're not coming in."

"Of course not." Tim fell into step behind her. "You didn't think I was hitting on you, did you?"

The thought had occurred to Dawn, especially after his compliment about her hair, but she kept her wild imaginings to herself. Of course Tim Hamilton wasn't hitting on her. It was ridiculous to think he might be interested in her when he had so many high-society glamour queens to choose from. As his administrative assistant, there wasn't a day went by that she didn't have to field at least one or two calls from women like that. It didn't matter that Tim rarely followed up on their invitations. They were still standing in line and waiting to go out with him whenever he was ready. That was all that counted.

The few minutes it took them to climb three flights of stairs to her apartment wasn't long enough for Dawn to quiet her nerves or settle her mind. She still had butterflies in her stomach when she reached her door, turned to face Tim and held out her hand. "Good night."

Belatedly, she realized what a mistake that normally inconsequential gesture was. Tim grasped her hand but instead of shaking it the way he would have if she'd been a man, he cradled her fingers gently and looked directly into her eyes. Dawn couldn't move, could hardly force herself to continue breathing.

"I want you to know how much I value the opportunity I had to make the rounds with you tonight," he said quietly, sincerely. "You gave me a new appreciation of the hard work so many volunteers do. I honestly had no idea."

She strained to pull her hand away and he reluctantly let go. "I'm glad you enjoyed it. And thanks for giving all that extra food from Betty's to the last family. I'm sure the Martins are grateful. They need all the help they can get, especially until Jordan's able to go back to work again."

"Glad to do it." Tim smiled. "You warned me I'd better not throw anything away and it seemed a logical alternative. I'm glad I was there to help you carry that heavy case of baby formula up those stairs for them. Do you usually lug it all that way yourself?"

"Sure. When I need to."

Tim stepped back and thrust his hands into the pockets of his slacks. "Well, you must be tired, so…"

"Exhausted," Dawn said. "Thanks for the ride."

He took another step away. "You're welcome."

Turning, she fumbled to get the key into the lock, finally succeeded, and started to duck into her apartment. Just as she did, something very substantial pushed past her legs without a sound.

All she had time to shout was, "Beau, no!" before the mastiff leaped and pinned Tim against the wall of the dimly lit hallway.

Dawn grabbed the dog's collar and tugged, yelling, "Beau! Down." He yielded easily.

To Tim she said, " Are you okay?"

"I think so." He was wiping his face and seemed short of breath.

"I'm so sorry. Beau's usually very good about staying inside. I didn't think he'd burst out like that. He must have heard my voice and…" *And sensed how nervous I am,* she finished silently.

The astonished expression lingering on Tim's

face made her grin in spite of the embarrassing situation. "Are you sure you're okay?"

"I think so. Boy, does he have bad breath!" Tim stared at the now-lethargic-looking animal seated at her feet and panting as if it had just chased down and captured a man-eating lion. "What is he?"

"A dog."

"I'd already figured out that part. What I mean is, what are you doing with an animal the size of an elephant in your little apartment? Does your landlord know?"

"Yes. I'm allowed to have one pet as long as the other neighbors aren't bothered by any noise. Beau's so quiet I doubt most of them even know he's here."

"Beau?"

"Short for Beauregard. A proper Southern name, don't you think? Beau was my brother's dog. After the terrible accident I told you about, Phil didn't want Mom to have to deal with caring for Beau, too, so he asked me to take him in."

"And, of course, you did."

"Sure. He's a wonderful companion. Very gentle."

Tim was brushing himself off as if contact with the mastiff had left him muddy. "I'll have to take your word for it. I haven't had much experience with dogs and such."

Dawn was aghast. "You never had a pet when you were a little boy?"

He shook his head. "I think the girls had some goldfish once. I can't remember for sure."

"That is so sad."

Shrugging, Tim continued to brush at his dark slacks. "Not to me, it isn't. We had plenty of other interests, like school and sports. I never felt I was missing anything by not having a dog shedding all over the furniture and chewing up my shoes."

"Well, you were," Dawn said.

She guided Beau toward the apartment door with a light touch on his collar and urged him to enter ahead of her. As she followed, she noted that Tim was still standing in the dim, narrow hallway, staring after her. His expression made her wonder if he was having trouble digesting her candid criticism of his childhood.

Probably. Tim wasn't very good at recognizing the wisdom of ideas that differed from his own, no matter how sensible they were. The Hamilton way was the only way, according to him, and, sadly, he usually refused to listen to any opinions to the contrary.

Dawn spent a restless night. She had belatedly come to the realization she didn't have a ride to work the following morning and had spent hours trying to decide what to do about it. No way was she going to ask Tim to come and get her. No, sir. Not after the way his compliment about her hair had shaken her up. And putting the whole incident out of her mind was beyond impossible. So she'd phoned her friend Gabi Valencia, and begged Gabi to give her a ride into Davis Landing on her way to her job at the hospital's administration office.

Gabi picked her up early, as Dawn had requested. "You should have called me yesterday, when you found out your car was out of commission," Gabi said. "I'd have helped you with the meals. There's plenty of room in my van."

Too weary to deal with the teasing she knew would ensue if she told Gabi everything, Dawn decided to hold back some of the details of her unsettling evening. She wrapped her light jacket more tightly around herself and held it there, her arms crossed. "I would have asked you, but I thought Talia had soccer practice on Monday nights."

"That's old news. Both my girls change their minds so often it drives me loca." She smiled over at Dawn. "So, how did it go with you and the boss man last night?"

Dawn's head snapped around. "How did you know he was involved?"

"Small town. Big, talkative church," Gabi said with a smile. "I probably knew who you were with before you made your first meal delivery."

"Probably. It was quite an evening."

"Bad?"

"Not exactly." Dawn was shaking her head slowly, pensively. "Tim—Mr. Hamilton—was a perfect gentleman. And he related well to the oldsters, especially Stuart Meyers."

"Whoa!" Gabi gave her a quizzical look. "*Tim?* Since when have you called him *that?*"

"Since last night when he told everybody at Northside, including me, to use his first name. I'm going to have to be really careful not to do it at work."

"Not necessarily. Maybe it's okay because the guy likes you. On a personal level, I mean."

"It wouldn't matter to me if he did. Timothy Hamilton is not the kind of man I'd ever consider forming any kind of relationship with. He's too— I don't know—stuffy? Rigid? Polished?"

"You forgot, *rich*. And powerful."

"Yeah. That's another problem. He has no idea what it's like to struggle to make ends meet, so he really can't relate to those of us who have. Does that make sense?"

"Completely. From what I've seen of him when he's come into the business office at the hospital, the guy is hard as nails. It's like he knows he could buy or sell any of us and have change left over, so he isn't worried about not getting his own way."

"That's exactly how I've always pictured him," Dawn said. "But for a while last night he seemed different. You should have seen him with Stuart Meyers. They were like two little boys playing toy soldiers. If I hadn't been pressed for time, I suspect they'd have reenacted the entire battle of Nashville."

"No kidding? That is amazing."

"It sure is." She stared out the window, unseeing, as they crossed the Cumberland River into Davis Landing on Mill Road and came to the corner of Main where the Hamilton Media building stood.

"You can just let me off out front," Dawn said. "I don't want to make you late."

Gabi laughed. "That's no problem today, kiddo. You got me up at the crack of *dawn,* no pun intended. I've got over an hour to kill before I'm due at the hospital." She pulled to a stop. "How's this?"

"Fine. Thanks." Dawn gathered up her purse and sack lunch and started to get out of the minivan.

Gabi laid a hand lightly on her arm. "Why was that?"

"Why was what?"

"The early call. The trip from your place to here takes less than twenty minutes, even when traffic is bad. Why did you ask me to pick you up at seven when you don't normally leave home till nearly eight?" She suddenly broke into a grin. "You were avoiding Tim Hamilton, weren't you? That's it. You didn't want him to be the one to pick you up. By leaving an hour early you cut your chances of being home if he did show."

"That's ridiculous." Dawn knew her reddening cheeks were giving away a truth she didn't want to admit, even to her best friend.

"It is not. I can see it in your eyes. Did he upset you or something? I thought you said he behaved like a perfect gentleman."

"He did. It's not him that I'm worried about. It's my reaction to him that scares me silly." Dawn swallowed hard and nervously licked her dry lips. "Miss Ada kept going on and on about how pretty I was and Tim agreed with her."

"So? What's so terrible about that?"

"It wasn't what he said, it was the way he said it." Dawn looked at her friend and heaved an audible sigh. "Unfortunately, he sounded like he meant every word."

Dawn was already hard at work when her boss burst into the office, tie and coattails flying. He gaped at her. "Where were you? I knocked and knocked. Your dog was barking like crazy. If one of your neighbors hadn't told me you weren't home I'd still be beating on your door and making a fool of myself—if the dog hadn't broken out and had me for breakfast, first."

"I'm sorry. When we left here yesterday you said you planned to come in early so I thought…"

Tim raked his fingers through his dark, wavy hair, leaving it slightly mussed. Dawn couldn't recall seeing him this agitated since Wallace's diagnosis of leukemia had been officially announced to the staff.

"Okay. Forget it," he said, visibly calming himself and regaining his characteristic air of unperturbed authority as he straightened his tie. "How about some coffee?"

"Sure." She got to her feet and started for the small kitchenette beside the washroom. "I just made a fresh pot."

"No. Not up here," Tim said. "Let's go over to Betty's where we can relax and talk."

"Betty's?" Dawn's voice squeaked so badly she was sure it had risen at least an octave.

"The Bakeshoppe and Bookstore? Right across the street? It's been there since 1941. The plaque on the wall says so."

He'd begun to smile, Dawn noted. Sort of. Actually, he was gazing at her as if he wondered where her wits had gone. Well, he wasn't the *only* one who wondered that!

"I know all about Betty's," she said cynically. "What I can't figure out is why you want to go there with me."

"Why not? I found out yesterday that your table manners are fine. Why wouldn't I want to eat with you?"

"That's not what I meant." Dawn had a terrible thought. Suppose he was planning to take her out of the office so he could let her down easy? "You—you aren't going to fire me, are you?"

"No, I'm not going to fire you. Come on. I haven't had anything to eat yet. I could really use a cup of coffee and a sweet roll."

She hesitated. "Well, I—"

"Look. Consider this an assignment if it will make you feel better. I want to discuss a few business ideas I've had since last night and I thought it would be more enjoyable if we could do it away from here."

"Business? You want to discuss business with *me?*"

He chuckled. "Yes, Ms. Leroux. I want to hear what you think about possible changes in the newspaper. Can you think of any reason why I shouldn't run them by you?"

"No. But if you're planning to try to out-do the *Observer,* I'm not sure talking about it at Betty's is a good idea. Nothing stays secret once it's reached the Bakeshoppe rumor mill."

"Point taken. We'll sit in the back and talk quietly, privately," Tim said with a grin. He nodded toward the door he'd just entered. "Come on. Let's get out of here before somebody shows up with a crisis that won't wait and keeps us from our breakfast."

Dawn wasn't surprised to see every head turn when they walked into the Bakeshoppe together. By this afternoon, local gossip would probably have them romantically involved. The idea sent a tingle zinging down her spine. Speaking of which, Tim had placed his hand at her back so gently she could hardly feel it, yet she knew without a doubt that it hovered there.

"You shivered," he said. "If you're chilly, let's sit away from the ceiling fans."

"Okay."

Dawn led the way past the old original bakery counter to a small round table tucked away in a far corner and slipped gracefully into one of the black-painted wooden chairs before he could pull it out for her.

Buffeted on two sides by shelves crammed with used books and topped with antique knickknacks, she folded her hands on the tabletop and regarded him seriously as he took his place across from her.

"I think it should be safe to talk back here,"

Dawn said, "as long as we don't speak too loudly." She would have continued if their waitress, Betty's older daughter, Justine, hadn't approached with two glasses of ice water and an expectant expression.

"Morning, folks." Justine pulled out a pencil and poised it over her order pad. "What can I get you?"

Tim looked at Dawn when he said, "Two coffees?"

She nodded.

"And a couple of cinnamon rolls. They smell delicious."

"That'll be fine," Dawn said.

Justine wrote rapidly. "Coming right up. How was that picnic lunch we fixed for you yesterday, Mr. Hamilton? Satisfactory?"

"Very good. The basket's in my car. I'll have Herman return it to you."

Dawn waited until their order had been delivered and they were once again alone before she said, "Okay. What's your idea? And why did we have to come over here to talk about it?"

"Partly because it's not a formal proposal. Not yet," he said. "I'd like to get your take on it before I go any further. Once I mention it to Ed Bradshaw he'll want to handle everything the same as he always did when Jeremy was running the show, and that's not what I have in mind."

"Really." She forked a bite of warm cinnamon roll into her mouth. "Umm, this is good. Go on."

"It came to me while I was talking to Stuart Meyers last night. Colorful characters like him are too often overlooked. Suppose we launched a weekly column featuring interviews with some of the old-timers, starting with Stuart? Do you think it would help the *Dispatch* stay more in touch with the interests of its subscribers?"

"I don't know about that, but it would sure please Stuart. He's always lamenting the lack of enthusiasm younger people have for history."

"Exactly. Do you think he'd be willing to grant an interview?"

"I don't see why not. Once he got started talking, the trick would probably be getting a word in edgewise to ask him questions."

"I know. That's why I want you to be the one to talk to him and write the first article."

Dawn choked on his suggestion and covered her mouth with her napkin until she could swallow. "Me?"

"Yes. You're a natural for the job. You already know him. And your background is in English. It's perfect."

She took a sip of her water, hoping to calm the nervous tickle that was threatening to close her throat. A dire conclusion had arisen. "You *are* firing me."

Tim shook his head and looked at her as if she were delusional. "No. I'm unfairly doubling your workload. Does that make you feel better?"

Swallowing more water to buy thinking time she realized he was serious. "You want me to do *both* jobs?"

"Just temporarily. After we run the first article

we'll see how it flies. If it's a success we'll assign a regular reporter to carry on."

"Temporarily," Dawn echoed. "I think I'm beginning to see. You want me to moonlight as a writer."

"Exactly."

"What if I'm no good?"

"Editors can fix anything," Tim assured her. "Just give it your best shot and we'll go from there. What do you say?"

"I say, I'm nuts to even consider it." She'd begun to smile slightly. "But it sounds like fun. Okay. I'll do it. When do you need the article?"

"Is two weeks too soon?" Tim asked.

She arched her eyebrows and rolled her eyes. "How should I know? I've never done anything like this before. I have no idea if I'll need two weeks or two months."

Chuckling quietly, Tim took another sip of his coffee. "Try to make it sooner than that, will you? When Dad gets back on his feet he may want to take over everything again. I'd like to have my innovations in place and be able to prove they're working before I get booted out on my ear."

"He would never do that to you."

"Why not? He did it to Jeremy—with help from the stress of his illness." Tim settled back in his chair, both hands wrapped around his nearly empty coffee mug, and stared at it as he spoke. "I know I'm doing a better job managing Hamilton Media than my brother did, but that doesn't mean Dad will see it that way. I've always had to prove myself to him. I still do."

Dawn didn't know what to say. To her relief, Tim swiveled in his chair and redirected his interest, acting ashamed that he'd admitted to having an Achilles' heel. "Where did that Justine go? We could use refills."

"I don't know. I see Betty over by the coffeemakers."

Tim waved politely, trying to catch the older woman's eye without success.

"Looks like she's really distracted this morning," Dawn remarked. "Something must be bothering her. She's usually the first one to jump up and make the rounds with a fresh pot."

Tim pushed away from the table, his cinnamon roll hardly touched. "It doesn't matter. I've had enough coffee, anyway. Take your time finishing. I'll pay the tab on the way out and meet you back at the office."

"Don't you ever relax?"

"Not when there's work to do."

"We both came in early today. I think we can afford to take the time to drink a second cup of coffee." She glimpsed Justine across the room and waved. This time, the silent summons worked. "Here she comes. See? You'll have your coffee in a sec. Now please, sit down and give me a few pointers on writing a feature article, will you? I'm already starting to be sorry I agreed to try."

"You're friendly with Felicity, aren't you? Ask for

her help. Just let her think you're working on a piece for a historical newsletter or something like that so she doesn't blab to Bradshaw before we're ready."

Dawn scowled at him. "Lie?"

"Well, no, not exactly. Just withhold the truth."

"That's the same thing as telling an outright lie."

"Who says?"

"The Bible." She studied his handsome face for some sign he recognized the biblical principle. If he did, it didn't register in his expression. "It warns against bearing false witness, for one thing. Besides the Ten Commandments, I think that's found in the thirteenth chapter of Romans."

"My mother and sisters handle all that religious stuff," Tim said. "I don't have time to fool with it."

"I'm sure I've seen your brother Chris at our Northside Community Church services, too. Recently, he's been coming with Felicity."

"I suppose he may go to church on the days he's off duty. Look, you can tell her as much as you feel you need to in order to get her help. Just caution her to keep it quiet, okay?"

"Okay."

Dawn accepted a belated coffee refill from Justine but Tim waved her off, tossed down money for the tip and left the table.

Watching him stride purposefully toward the exit, Dawn was struck by how terribly alone he must feel. His father, Wallace, who had been in charge of the Hamilton Media dynasty, was still ailing and might die from complications of the treatment meant to cure him. Nora, Tim's mother, spent most of her time and energy at her husband's side. Jeremy, Tim's eldest brother, had left town after what had been reported by office gossips as a terrible family quarrel, and his baby sister had run off with her no-good boyfriend at a time when it looked like the Hamilton family was coming apart at the seams, which it apparently was, if Tim's attitude was any indication.

Setting Tim even further away from the others, his siblings were apparently connected, heart and soul, to a faith he openly rejected. Poor guy. If ever there was a man who had earned the title of "Loner," it was Tim Hamilton.

Justine returned to the coffeemakers, ostensibly to refill her glass pot, and confronted Betty. "Okay, Mom. He's gone. You can come out and go back to work now."

"I *am* working." She pushed back a stray wisp of graying hair and turned to rinse her plump hands in the sink.

"You know what I mean," Justine countered. "What's gotten into you?"

"Nothing. I just had things to do over here."

Justine blew a quiet raspberry her mother's way. "Phooey. You've been getting weirder every day, especially lately. You can't expect me to keep waiting on every Hamilton who comes in here all by myself. Sooner or later, someone will notice how you've been avoiding them."

"I don't avoid them. Not exactly. I just prefer to have someone else take their orders."

"Like me?" Justine's mouth pressed into a thin line. "If it bothers you, think how *I* must feel. Have Wendy do it if you don't want to. Just give me a break, okay?"

Betty looked surprised at her eldest daughter's outburst. "Your sister's busy in the kitchen."

Justine stood firm, shaking her head in disbelief. "I don't care. After what you told me about you and Wallace, how do you expect me to behave naturally around any of them? Huh? We work ourselves practically to death keeping this place running while guys like Tim Hamilton sit up in their fancy offices across the street and look down on folks like us, literally and figuratively."

"They do not!"

"Oh, yeah?" Upset, Justine failed to lower her voice when she said, "Wallace sure looked down on *you*."

"Justine! Hush! Someone will hear."

"Maybe it's time somebody did so we can quit pretending," the tall, slim, thirty-year-old said. "You and Wendy look alike. Dad was short, too. You know what the *Observer* article insinuated. How long do you think it's going to be before somebody takes a good look at me and imagines a family resemblance?"

"We don't know for sure," Betty insisted.

Justine sighed. "Yes, we do. You may want to keep lying to yourself but I've had all the positive proof I need. Accept it, Mom. Your biggest mistake is standing right here, waiting tables in your restaurant."

Reaching for her daughter's hand, Betty grasped it tightly. "Don't ever think that, Justine. Never. I wouldn't trade you for anything. You know that. You must. If Daddy was alive, I know he'd say the same thing." Tears had filled her eyes. "I love you, baby. I wish I could change things but I can't, so we'll have to live with it. I'm so sorry."

"Yeah," Justine said, penitent and equally teary-eyed. "I'm sorry, too. Guess I was thinking of myself too much. It's just that every time I see one of the Hamiltons these days, I get kind of crazy."

"Now that's something I can fix," her mother said. "From now on, if I'm available, I'll wait on them."

"It's okay. I can keep doing it."

Betty shook her head, her expression resolute. "No. It wasn't fair of me to push it off on you in the first place. I just wasn't thinking clearly. When I heard them talking about how Wallace was failing, I guess it all boiled up inside me, that's all. I can cope, now. Honest. Like the Bible says, 'I can do all things through Christ.'"

"Tell you what," Justine said, forcing a smile and swiping at the tears trickling down her cheeks. "We'll do it together. Just like we always have. You, me and Wendy, all for one and one for all."

Across the room, inquisitive eyes watched the mother and daughter embrace and found the sight interesting, to say the least. Most of what they had been discussing had been muted by the noises of the other diners and the piped-in background music, but a few words had come through. Clearly, the Hamilton family was involved in whatever had upset Betty and her daughter. That alone was enough to make the listener rejoice.

Chapter Five

Tim was away from his desk when Dawn got a call that the repair garage had located a rental car for her and was bringing it over, so she grabbed her purse in case she needed identification and left her boss a note of explanation before she went downstairs to take delivery.

This time, she dutifully signed the lobby roster for Herman Gordon while Louise looked on approvingly.

"You 'spect to be gone long, Miss Dawn?" the old man asked. "Case somebody wants to know."

"No. Not long." She smiled at the elderly couple. They'd been with Hamilton Media for so many years, in one role or another, they were practically part of the scenery, like the bricks that made up the walls. If something happened to either of them, the old building would never seem quite as sturdy.

"I'm taking delivery of a rental car," Dawn explained.

Herman nodded. "That was some dent you got in your sedan, wasn't it? Yes, sirree. Good thing Mr. Wallace wasn't here to see what went on."

Dawn knew it was inappropriate to discuss her boss's shortcomings with the guards, no matter how long their tenure. "Accidents happen," she told him. "I'll be in the employee parking lot if anyone needs me."

That said, she spun on her heel, headed for the exit and ran smack into Tim Hamilton. He was standing outside the heavy, glass, revolving door, apparently preparing to enter.

He paused and gave her a quizzical look. "Where are you going, to interview Stuart?"

"No. Someone from the garage is bringing me wheels and I want to see what I—I mean what you— are paying for. I've never rented a car before so I really don't know what to expect. The rate they quoted me over the phone sounded pretty expensive."

"I told you it doesn't matter."

"I know, but…" She started past him, hoping he'd continue with whatever he'd been on his way to do. Instead, he fell into step beside her.

"I hope it doesn't look too good," Tim quipped. "I know how you hate nice cars."

Dawn made a face at him. "The cars are fine. It's the pretense I don't care for."

"The way I look at it," he drawled, "it's only a pretense if you can't afford it and are putting on airs. A good car is a tool of the trade, like anything else."

"Not to me, it isn't," she argued. "It's a survival necessity."

They'd reached the employee parking lot and paused. Apparently, the rental was still on its way because there were no extra vehicles in evidence. Dawn folded her jacket close in front and crossed her arms.

Tim struck a nonchalant pose. "Well, at least you'll have wheels for your meal deliveries tonight."

"Tomorrow night," she countered. "I deliver on Mondays and Wednesdays, remember?"

"That's right. You did say that, didn't you? Have you given any thought to writing the feature article we discussed?"

Dawn huffed. "That's all I have thought about. I'm afraid I'm in way over my head."

"I don't think so. When I was little, Dad used to tell me tough jobs were just like eating an elephant. If you tried to do it all at once, you'd fail, but if you took it one bite at a time, no job was too big."

She smiled, remembering. "My father used to say that was the way to eat a whale. I guess the difference was the Gulf coast influence."

"Guess so." He shifted his weight, giving her the impression he was anxious to be on his way.

"You don't have to stand here with me and waste your afternoon," Dawn said. "Go back to work. I left at least seven phone messages on your desk. Every caller swore his problem was a matter of life and death."

"That important, huh?" Tim smiled at her. "Okay. If you're sure you want to get rid of me, I'll go. Just promise you won't be too fussy about the car, whatever it looks like. We were lucky to get one at all."

"As long as it runs well enough to get me home and back, plus my meal deliveries, I'll be happy."

She was watching him walk away when a sleek black convertible with a flawless, mirror finish and more chrome than Felicity's '59 Caddy cruised into the parking lot and headed straight for her. That *couldn't* be her rental car, could it? The thing was glittering like a Mardi Gras parade float!

The young, long-haired driver, wearing a baseball cap and coveralls, stopped the car and held up a clipboard. "You Dawn Le…something?"

"Leroux," she said. "Yes. That's me."

"Then this here is your buggy." Climbing out, he handed her the key ring as a pickup truck pulled in behind them. "There's my ride." He shoved the clipboard at her. "Sign here, lady."

"But, that's, that's—"

"A fine set of wheels, if I do say so myself." He pushed a pen into her hand.

"I can't accept it."

The driver rolled his eyes. "What's the matter? Wrong color?"

"No, it's…"

She was trying to come up with a logical explanation when Tim appeared behind her, took the clipboard and scrawled his signature boldly across the form.

The driver, shaking his head as if he couldn't believe anyone would hesitate to accept delivery of such a fine, high-performance vehicle, climbed into the pickup truck and rode away.

Dawn spun to face Tim. "You knew, didn't you?"

"Knew what? That you were getting a car? Sure. You told me, remember?"

"You know what I mean. This is not just a car. It's an *expensive* car."

"Very." He was smiling. "So?"

"So, what did you have to do, *buy* it?"

"Let's just say the Hamilton influence has handy fringe benefits. If driving it embarrasses you, blame me."

The keys were clenched so tightly in her hand they were making dents in her palm. She lowered her voice and tried to appeal to his softer side. "I don't belong in that car, Tim. Look at it. It's gorgeous."

"Yeah, it kind of is, isn't it?" He eyed the cloudy sky. "Tell you what. Let's figure out how to put the top up, for starters. Then we can cruise around the parking lot together till you get the feel of it."

The first thing that popped into her mind was his recent misadventure in that very lot. "I don't think practicing anything in these narrow aisles is a very good idea. That's how we got into this mess in the first place, remember?"

He held up both hands, palms out, in mock surrender. "Don't worry. I promise never to drive while juggling a cell phone again. I've already ordered one of those remote speaker units for my car."

Opening the passenger door he stepped back and said, "You might as well get in because this is your car—at least for a while."

She pulled a face and sighed. "You don't intend to give up, do you?"

"Nope. It's not in my nature. You, of all people, should know that."

Resigned and a little miffed to have been placed in such an untenable position, Dawn circled the convertible, tossed her purse onto the backseat, put on her sunglasses and slid behind the wheel.

"All right. We'll do this your way, Mr. Hamilton. Get in, fasten your seat belt and hang on. If I'm going to drive this car, I'm really going to *drive* it."

To say that Tim was surprised in the next few minutes was an understatement. Dawn handled the sporty coupe as if she'd trained at a school for race drivers.

"I could have executed a tighter turn if this car had rear-wheel drive," she said, speaking loud enough to be heard over the roar of the engine and the air whooshing over the top rim and around the open sides of the windshield. "It handles pretty well, though."

Tim's eyes were wide, his hair tousled by the airstream. "Where did you learn to drive, Indianapolis?"

"Close." Grinning, she kept her eyes on the road. "Remember I told you about my brother? Phil didn't only speed on the motorcycle he wrecked, he was getting into racing stock cars professionally at the time he was hurt. He taught me how to handle a car at high speeds."

"He sure did!"

She laughed. "Would you like to drive now?"

"No thanks. I'm probably shaking too much for that. Drop me off at the office, will you?"

That brought another laugh. "You can't kid me. I know you too well to believe you're scared."

"How about apprehensive?"

"That, I can accept. Okay. Back to work for both of us. The gossips are probably already busy spreading the word about our little excursion on company time. No sense giving them more to talk about."

Tim nodded and sobered. "Yeah. The way that scandal sheet, the *Observer,* loves to dig up dirt on my family, you could find yourself pictured on page one."

"Nope. I haven't broken a single law. I'm very careful about things like that. My reputation is important to me."

"So is ours. But that didn't stop someone from revealing the dirt on Jeremy, no matter how much it hurt my mother. Have you seen the latest drivel? They've now started insinuating that Dad is hiding skeletons in our family closet, too."

"You mean the Media Mogul's Love Child article? I saw it. And the *Observer* didn't hesitate to print such trash. That's what's so cruel. I can't imagine who would lie about your father like that, can you?"

"No. If I knew, you'd better believe I'd put a

stop to it. I did talk to Richard McNeil about suing. He says if we take the *Observer* to court and it turns out they can prove even one of their allegations, we'll look like fools."

"Surely, they can't."

"I don't want to take that chance. It might give people the idea we're only fighting them because we print a rival newspaper. I want the *Dispatch* to prosper because it's a good paper, not because we're in some sham war with that despicable rag."

"Well said." Dawn wheeled into the Hamilton Media lot and brought the car to a smooth stop. "I'll drop you here and go park."

"Fine." Tim got out, then turned and leaned down with his elbows on the rim of the passenger door. "Can I ask you something? Considering the expert way you drive, why did you say you were afraid to borrow my BMW?"

"Because I was," she answered honestly. "There's a world of difference between a rental car and the boss's private wheels. I happen to like working here."

"You think I'd fire you for scratching a fender?"

"Well…"

"You *do* think that, don't you?" He straightened. "I can see my image needs almost as much improvement as this company does. From now on, I want you to bring it to my attention whenever you think I'm being insensitive."

Dawn's hands tightened on the wheel. "Me?"

"Who better to point it out?" Tim took a step

back and nodded. "You're the one who hates lies, so I'll expect nothing less than brutal honesty."

Her murmured, "Oh, brother," as she pulled away was lost in the roar of the engine. *Brutal honesty?* She couldn't do that. Not to Tim. He had enough problems without having his right hand-man—woman—attacking his character at every turn. Who did he think she was, his shrink?

No. He thinks I'm the only one who will tell him the truth, she concluded, *and he's probably right.* That was a high compliment. All she had to do was figure out how to help him without hurting him in the process.

She knew her free expression could prove a shock to a man who was used to having everything done his way. But it could also benefit him, as long as she tempered her words with kindness.

An overwhelming urge to protect Tim, even from herself, arose. Now *that* was a real surprise.

Living room lights were still on at Stuart Meyers's house when Dawn pulled up in front of it later that evening. She'd thought about phoning ahead but had decided it would be best if she proposed their interview and explained her assign-ment face-to-face.

She didn't know how many times she'd had to talk herself into continuing with this project. She'd even rehearsed a speech to her boss, declining the job she'd accepted on a whim. What had she been thinking? She was no feature writer.

Long ago, when she'd asked the Lord to help her resume her studies of English, she hadn't dreamed He might answer this way. Could this situation truly be answered prayer? Or was it merely coincidence that she was imagining as more important than it really was?

Dawn's logical side argued that she'd simply stumbled into the writing assignment by virtue of her regular employment. Then again, she argued, how much had God had to do with getting her the job at a place that published both a magazine and a newspaper in the first place?

Shaking off her fruitless introspection, she approached Stuart Meyers's front door and was surprised to hear what sounded like a loud movie on television. Either that, or World War III had started in his living room!

She rapped on the door the way she always did. No one answered. She knocked louder. Still nothing. Finally, she convinced herself the old man might be sick or injured and tried the knob.

The door swung open effortlessly and she peered in. "Mr. Meyers? Are…?"

She froze. Her mouth gaped. Across the room, Stuart and Tim Hamilton were staging the battle of Nashville on that big table, with all the gusto of two teenagers enjoying a noisy video game. What she'd assumed was a movie score was actually a tape of the *1812 Overture,* complete with cannon fire, playing so loudly in the background it rattled the windows. The house smelled faintly of oregano and garlic, like after-hours at an Italian restaurant.

Stuart looked up from his game and displayed a small plastic figure. "Dawn! Come on in. Look what the boy brought me! Horses. Got the whole cavalry."

Her gaze settled on Tim. He looked as pleased as the old man. Maybe more so. If his grin had spread any farther she imagined it would have wiggled his ears.

Tim laughed. "Close your mouth, Ms. Leroux. I told you I keep my promises. Come over here. We need somebody to be General Hood."

Grinning, she laid aside her notebook and purse and complied. "Okay, as long as it's Hood. My daddy would have a conniption if he found out I was pretending to be a Yankee general. What do I do?"

Tim caught her eye for an instant and raised his eyebrows. Clearly, he didn't know as much about the skirmish as Stuart did but he was doing his best to participate.

"We need more cannons! Bring on the fusiliers!" Stuart shouted. "Boom, boom! Gotcha."

"Where's Hood?" Dawn asked.

Tim had rolled up his shirtsleeves and shed his usual tie as well as his suit jacket. He pointed. "There. Right, Stuart?"

"Right, boy. He's advancing on General Thomas. Look out! Here comes more grapeshot! Nasty stuff. Takes out a whole line." With a flick of his fingers he knocked down a knot of a dozen plastic soldiers.

"I used to belong to a group of reenacters, you know, before this bum leg started givin' me fits. Had the whole authentic outfit, uniform, saber and everything."

"Which group?" Dawn asked, thinking of the article she was planning to write.

"I was a captain in the Tennessee Volunteers," the old man said proudly. "Most folks don't realize. There wasn't no standing army. Not like we have nowadays. Both sides were manned by volunteers that represented their hometowns and states. They provided their own uniforms, too, especially the officers. And guns, them that had 'em. That's why there wasn't no good way to keep 'em supplied. Too many different kinds of rifles and pistols, some muzzle-loading, some not. The right cartridges were pure gold to a fightin' man."

Looking to Tim, Stuart grinned. "Say, son, you don't happen to know where I can get a real cannon, do you? Not a big one. Just a little popgun to make smoke, like they do when a fuse burns down to the black powder."

Tim laughed. "I'm not sure that's a good idea. I was glad to bring you some cavalry, but I can just see you shooting a hole in your house if I gave you a real cannon."

That tickled the old man. "Just met me and already he thinks he knows me that well." He winked at Dawn, then looked a bit surprised and began to frown. "Say, what brings you here? It's not Wednesday. I may be old but I still have a good memory. You were just here last night. This has to be Tuesday."

"It is," she said. Thinking about asking Stuart for an interview made her suddenly nervous and she licked her dry lips. "I'm, um, here on business. Sort of. My boss has asked me to write about interesting people for the *Davis Landing Dispatch*."

"And you picked me?" He cackled. "What's so interesting about an old codger with a bum leg and a living room full of toy soldiers?"

"Your hobby of re-creating history, for one thing," she said. "And I'd like to hear more about your life. Where you came from, what brought you here, how long you've lived in this house, things like that."

"Why? Nobody'd be interested."

"Yes, they would." She looked to Tim for support. "We are, aren't we?"

He nodded. "Actually, Stuart, it was my idea for Dawn to kick off our new feature with you. Think about it for a second. You care what people did, what kinds of lives they led, over a hundred and fifty years ago. Why wouldn't others be interested in hearing your story?"

The old man's gnarled fingers grasped the tiny figure of a mounted cavalry officer and held it up. "Because these men made a real difference. They may have been on opposite sides but they were all doing what they thought was right."

"Like you and my grandfather were doing when you enlisted to fight in World War II?" Tim asked.

"Ah, we were just a couple of naive kids. We survived more by sheer coincidence than by our wits." Staring across the room as if in a daze, he began to smile wistfully. "My Ellie always said she'd got me through that war on her knees. I suppose she did do a powerful lot of prayin'. Most folks did. Ellie and me, we got married as soon as I got back to the States."

He blinked, clearing his vision, and looked at Dawn. "She was a good woman, my Ellie. Can I tell you about her? Will you put her in your story?"

"Of course," Dawn said tenderly. "This is supposed to be a personal interest feature. You can tell me anything you want to and I'll do my best to see that it appears in the paper. How about pictures? Do you have any old ones you'd like to share?"

He snapped out of his reverie, jumped up and grabbed his cane. "You betcha. Got a slew of 'em. Wait there. I'll be right back."

"Good job," Tim said, verbally patting her on the back after Stuart hobbled out of the room. "Got him. I knew you could do it."

She cast a wry smile at her self-satisfied-looking boss. "I got an interview and maybe some pictures. That doesn't make an article. I still have to write it all down and organize it so it makes sense."

"You can do it," he said with a sidelong glance at the war games table. "Any general who can command an entire army division can certainly sort out the details of one little newspaper article."

If anyone other than Tim Hamilton had teased her like that, Dawn would have immediately made a face and playfully smacked his arm. She thought about doing it anyway. In the end, sensibility won out and she merely set her jaw.

Such displays of informal camaraderie in regard to Tim were more than unwise, she reminded herself. They were foolhardy. Not only was she already forgetting her place and calling him by his first name more often than she liked, she was also beginning to picture him as a potential friend—or more.

That would never do.

Timothy Hamilton was her boss, period. He wasn't her buddy, or her cohort, or her meals-on-wheels fellow volunteer. And he certainly wasn't her boyfriend, even if her imagination did try to assign him that ridiculous fantasy role whenever she let her guard down.

Then again, Tim wasn't as stuffy and unapproachable as she'd originally thought, either. Dawn huffed silently. Life had certainly been easier before he'd hit her car and she'd found out he had a human side, hadn't it?

And speaking of cars. Frowning, she stared at him. "Hey. I didn't notice your silver BMW when I drove up. How did you get here?"

"My car's in the shop, too. I dropped it off this afternoon and the dealership gave me a loaner. It's parked a few doors up the street."

"Why didn't you drive your Ferrari?"

"Logistics," Tim said. "It was at home. I wasn't

sure how late Stuart stayed up and I didn't want to take the extra time to trade vehicles. I may drive it to work in the morning."

"Oh." She didn't like admitting that she might have turned around and gone home without ever coming in if she'd suspected that Tim was there, but it was true. This interview promised to be difficult enough without adding the distraction his presence brought.

Stuart returned with a photo album just in time to save Dawn from having to make more small talk. Relieved, she settled on the worn, floral fabric-covered sofa next to the old man and began to take notes while he talked about his fascinating life.

It would have been a lot easier to concentrate on the task at hand if she hadn't sensed that Tim was watching her from across the room, obviously assessing her interviewing style and evaluating her skills. Or lack of them.

She couldn't believe how hard it was to keep from looking up and making eye contact with him. If she hadn't had Stuart's story to concentrate on she didn't think she could have held out as long as she did.

Finally, she lifted her lashes and peeked over at Tim. The supportive smile he bestowed upon her seemed so warm and genuine it sent a tingle of elation singing up her spine and tickled the hair at the nape of her neck.

"You get that last part?" Stuart asked her. "You stopped writin'."

Dawn blinked to clear her head. "Um, I think so. You were talking about D-day, right?"

"Right."

Approaching, Tim offered his hand as he spoke to Stuart. "I've enjoyed our evening but I really should be getting on home. You two relax and finish your business. I'll see myself out."

"Don't forget that cannon," the old man gibed, briefly shaking hands. "I'll be lookin' for it."

"I imagine you will."

"And bring another pizza like you did tonight. An army can't fight on an empty stomach, you know. I'm partial to sausage. No olives. They give me heartburn something fierce."

Chuckling and shaking his head, Tim bid them both a good-night, turned away and headed for the door.

"You don't really expect him to buy you a working cannon, do you?" Dawn asked as soon as she and Stuart were alone.

"Don't know. He might. It don't hurt to ask. He sure surprised me when he showed up tonight with all them horses and such."

"Yeah," she said softly, "he surprised me, too."

Chapter Six

Tim Hamilton's penthouse encompassed the entire top floor of The Enclave, Davis Landing's most prestigious address. His sister Amy had a smaller apartment in the same six-story building, as did Jeremy, although he hadn't been home in ages.

Absently greeting The Enclave's night guard, Tim stepped into the elevator and used his key to unlock the controls, giving him access to his private floor.

How long was Jeremy going to stay away? Tim wondered as the elevator hummed and rose smoothly. *No telling.* The angry way they'd parted still grated on his conscience. He'd overreacted. They both had.

In view of the stress surrounding Wallace's ongoing illness, there was no guarantee things would be different the next time they met, either, but Tim hoped he'd be able to moderate his own feelings enough to bring a semblance of peace. He owed it to his mother to try.

Their mother, he corrected. He and Jeremy might have different fathers but they still shared Nora. And she needed all her children around her in harmony at a time like this, which was further reason to be irritated with his older brother. Though Jeremy had phoned home several times since he'd gone searching for his true grandparents, he seemed oblivious to anyone else's needs. Of all the things Jeremy had said and done, cutting himself off from the family at a time like this was, in Tim's considered opinion, the absolute worst.

The elevator stopped on the top floor, the doors slid quietly open, and Tim stepped into the marble-floored foyer of his apartment. *Home.* He paused, taking it in. The place was almost too quiet. After his chaotic visit to Stuart's—and the earlier attack by Dawn's monster dog—all this peacefulness seemed a bit like an anticlimax.

In keeping with the style of the rest of the building and his personal aversion to anything fussy, his furniture was sleek and modern. Expensive. Spotless. Except for a couple of bright throw pillows his sister Amy had insisted he add to the decor, the whole place was a plain black and white and gray. What natural wood there was, was the finest, hand-rubbed teak. So few footsteps had crossed the living room, the paths of the maid's vacuum cleaner were visible on the thick, ivory carpet in a random, overlapping, geometric design.

In the past, Tim had judged the place ideal. Now, it seemed too sterile, too perfect. He crossed to the glass door and walked out onto the balcony over-looking Sugar Tree Park.

The air was cool and crisp, hinting at winter's approach. Moonlight reflected off the glassy surface of the lake below, enhancing the starkness of Tim's world. In the daytime, the park seemed warm and welcoming with its green lawns, shady knolls and clusters of fall flowers. Looking at it at night seemed to bring out its more somber side, a side he had never before noticed.

"What's the matter with me," he muttered. "This place is exactly what I've always wanted. It's got everything. *I've* got everything."

Except...? his heart asked.

Except, nothing, he answered flatly. *I'm just overtired. The stress of work and Dad's illness is getting to me, that's all.*

Deciding that what he needed was useful distraction, he went back inside, took his briefcase into the den and opened it on his desk. There was plenty to do if a man put his mind to it. Hard work would fix whatever ailed him. It always had before.

Dawn telephoned her best friend, Gabi Valencia, as soon as she got home. "Hi. I hope I'm not calling too late. I didn't want to wake the girls."

Gabi stifled a yawn. "Too late? Naw, those kids could sleep through a hurricane. I'm glad you woke me. I'd fallen asleep in my chair and it's time I went to bed like normal people."

"I'm sorry. I just needed to hear a friendly

voice. Would it be better if I called back another time?"

Gabi chuckled softly. "No. *No hay problema,* as my *mamacita* always says. What makes you need a buddy at this time of night?" She yawned. "What time is it, anyway?"

"Just after ten. Listen, remember the writing job for the *Dispatch* I told you about?"

"The feature? Sure. What about it?"

"I went over to Stuart Meyers's house and interviewed him tonight."

"Okay. So?"

"So, Tim—Mr. Hamilton was there."

"Whoa. Start over. I don't think I understood. Your boss was *where?*"

"At Stuart's. I couldn't believe it, either. Not only was he there, on his own, he'd brought a pizza for them to share and had presented Stuart with the cutest set of toy soldiers. On horseback."

"Tim rode a *horse?*"

"No, silly." Dawn laughed. "The toys were cavalrymen. You know. The guys they used to call horse soldiers?"

"Let me get this straight. Tim Hamilton—*your* Tim Hamilton—was playing war with Stuart Meyers and there was no profit in it? Amazing!"

"That's what I thought," Dawn said. "He couldn't have known I was planning to stop by. Even I didn't know it when I left work. I'd been thinking about phoning Stuart to ask if I could do the piece on his life when it occurred to me that it would be better to ask him in person. When I showed up over there, he and Tim were already playing like a couple of kids." She paused and sighed. "Actually, it was kind of cute."

Beau was leaning against her leg, begging for affection, so she reached down and ruffled his ears.

Gabi snorted. "Repeat after me, 'Tim Hamilton is not cute.'"

"Can't do it," Dawn said. "He was adorable."

"The closest that man ever got to being adorable was probably while he was still sleeping in a crib and living on baby formula."

"Yeah, well…"

"Listen *amiga*," Gabi said, "this whole conversation is absurd. You know it and I know it. Get your head back on straight and forget about liking your boss. An attitude like that will bring you nothing but grief."

"What if I can't help it?" Dawn asked.

"Then you obviously need your head examined and that's far beyond my expertise. Just promise me you won't go and do anything stupid."

"Like what?"

"Like fall in love when there's no hope of a happy ending."

"Hey! I just said I was starting to *like* Tim, not that I was falling in love with him."

"That's how it starts," Gabi warned. "I ought to know. I never saw anything but a rosy future when I married Ostin Valencia and now look at me."

"You're doing a wonderful job raising your girls by yourself," Dawn offered. "Roni and Talia are great kids. If it hadn't been for Octavio, whatever his faults, you wouldn't have them."

"True enough. I just don't want to see you hurt, that's all. Promise me you'll take your time and think things through. I don't want you getting in so deep you flounder and maybe drown."

The water analogy struck Dawn funny. "I promise, *mamacita.* I'll always wear my water-wings and wade in with a buddy, like you, holding my hand." She giggled nervously.

"You'd better, kiddo," her friend replied. "Because it looks to me like you're already swimming with the sharks. You just haven't spotted their dorsal fins yet."

Laughing, Dawn bid Gabi a fond goodbye and hung up. She didn't think she'd taken the advice to heart till she found herself humming the theme from the scary movies about being eaten alive by a great white!

Predictably, Tim was already hard at work when Dawn got to the office the following day. She greeted him with a cheery, "Good morning."

"Morning." He barely looked up.

There was a half-empty coffee mug on the desk near his right elbow. Dawn eyed it. "Is that fresh?"

"No. It's yesterday's. But I didn't want to stop and make a new pot."

"Yuck." She took the mug to the sink and rinsed it out, then disposed of the thick brown sludge in the coffeemaker. "I don't know how anybody can drink day-old coffee. It's sickening."

"It was all I had," Tim muttered, still concentrating on the spreadsheets he'd been studying when she'd arrived.

Nodding as if he'd made an important decision, he leaned back in his chair. "Come here and have a look at this. I don't want you to say anything to the staff yet, but you'll need to know. I'm going to outsource our bookkeeping like my dad wanted."

Dawn's breath caught. Her eyes widened. "You mean you're going ahead with the contract Jeremy refused to sign, even after your father insisted?"

"Yes." Tim pointed to the green-tinted sheets of figures on his desk. "There's no doubt it's best for business."

"I see." She hesitated, then squared her shoulders and spoke boldly. "You told me to tell you when your public image needed work. Well, this is one of those times."

"Go on." He laced his fingers behind his head.

"There's nothing wrong with being mad at your brother because he let Curtis Resnick get away with embezzlement and didn't want to prosecute him for the sake of their friendship. I happen to think that was a stupid decision, too, especially because Curtis is still hanging around Davis Landing and bragging about what fools he thinks the Hamiltons are. The problem is, you'll be putting innocent people out of a job if you sign that contract."

"That's where you come in," Tim said calmly, lowering his arms and leaning his elbows on the desk. "I want you to find them slots within

Hamilton Media, if you can. If not, we'll make sure they have good jobs outside before we make any permanent changes. That was why I wanted their personnel files updated."

"Oh. Oh, well then…"

He snorted a wry chuckle. "There's no need to blush, Ms. Leroux. I admire your honesty. I'd told you to sound off if you thought I was making a mistake and you did. That's nothing to be ashamed of."

"Still, I apologize. I should have known what you were thinking when I saw which employee files you wanted to see. I think most of those people will fit into other areas, except maybe the department head. Bob is pretty much a human calculator and not very versatile. We may have to find him something else."

"Fine."

"And speaking of being versatile," Dawn said. "I've almost finished that article about Stuart Meyers."

"I'm looking forward to reading it. Have you got it with you?"

"No. I—um—I thought I was supposed to give it to an editor."

"I'd like to see it first."

Rats. She was afraid he'd say that. "Well, I guess I could bring in the rough draft. But I'd rather have it polished up before I share it with anyone." *Especially you.*

In the background, the coffeemaker was noisily burbling and dribbling, inspiring her to add, "While you're reading it, I want you to keep in mind how great my coffee tastes."

Tim frowned above a lopsided grin. "I'm afraid you've lost me."

"In case you don't like my writing? I don't want to be looking for another job, too, so I thought I should remind you of something good about myself."

It was Tim's turn to be nonplussed. He swiveled his chair and got to his feet. "I don't have to be reminded. There isn't a day goes by that I don't thank God for an able, trustworthy assistant like you."

She was astounded. "Do you mean that?"

"Every word."

"Even the part about thanking God?"

Tim arched an eyebrow and nodded slowly, thoughtfully, before he turned toward the window and answered with his back to her, "Yes. Even that."

Dawn figured she wouldn't have one original phrase left in her article if she edited it much more. Rather than compose directly onto a computer, she preferred to see the words on paper, but her first draft was getting so scribbled up it was almost impossible to read. Therefore, she'd either have to recopy the whole thing in longhand or return to the office computer to input the changes, then reprint.

She opted to use the computer so she could also get an accurate word count and see how—and if— the sentences flowed. Since it was Saturday, she knew she'd have the whole Hamilton building to herself and could bide her time getting everything just right, even if it took all evening.

A pot of homemade vegetable beef soup with a touch of Louisiana spice had been simmering on a back burner at her apartment. Rather than leave it cooking unattended and risk a fire—or trust Beau not to give in to his natural instincts and stick his nose where it didn't belong—Dawn decided to take her supper to the office with her. Then, she reasoned, if she decided to stay late she'd have something good to eat. Betty's Bakeshoppe café closed early and Dawn had gone hungry more than once when she'd worked past 6:00 p.m. and lost track of time.

She stuffed her article into her purse and grabbed the quilted cozy she often used to transport hot dishes to church suppers. It was a little small for the pot of soup but it would do if she wrapped and tied it tightly. And it would keep any drips from damaging her expensive rental car if the pot happened to leak past its lid. Boy, would she be relieved when she finally got her old car back.

Bidding a sorrowful-looking Beau goodbye, she slipped out the door and shut it behind her with a thrust of one hip rather than set the pot on the floor.

All the way to the office she mulled over the article about Stuart. She'd read those sentences so many times they were committed to memory. That was not good. Objectivity was impossible if she knew the work too well.

Approaching Hamilton Media she ignored the

driveway to the employee parking lot. Nobody would care if she left her car where the VIPs usually parked. None of them would be here, anyway. Except…

"Uh-oh." Dawn's heart sped. One Hamilton was here. A car was in his assigned spot. She searched her memory. Had Tim mentioned that he might come in to work over the weekend? She didn't recall his actually saying so but a shadow of doubt lingered in the back of her mind. He might have said something about it. And her subconscious might have responded by causing her to bring enough food to feed them both. If not, having a whole pot of soup with her was certainly fortuitous.

She supposed she could turn her rental car around and go home but she really didn't want to do that. Nor did she feel it would be wrong to stay. There was always a guard on duty so she and Tim wouldn't be in the building unchaperoned, and besides, maybe he'd just left the car there and ridden to the hospital to visit Wallace with Amy or some other member of his family.

"Right, Dawn," she murmured sarcastically, "and pigs can fly, too. The man is here and you know it."

Of course he was. And she found she was looking forward to going upstairs and seeing him, sharing her supper with him. Tim seldom remembered to eat when he was working. It would do him good to have a decent, home-cooked meal.

She began to smile as she started toward the entrance. This trip would have been a good idea even if she'd had the sense to consciously plan it. Tim needed food, she needed to work on her article in the peaceful atmosphere of a nearly deserted office and she made some of the tastiest, heartiest soup in the South. What could be better?

The part-time guard saw her approaching and opened the door for her. She greeted him. "Evening, Sam. How's it going?"

"Great, Ms. Dawn." His nose twitched. "Hoo-whee, that smells good. What is it?"

"Homemade soup, Louisiana style. I'm taking it to Mr. Hamilton. I assume he's here?"

"Yup. Been up there nearly all day, according to the sign-in sheet. That man's a workin' fool."

"You can say that again." She suppressed a chuckle. "Come on up and eat with us if you like. I brought plenty."

The guard touched the brim of his cap and held the elevator door for her while he pushed the proper button. "Thank you, ma'am. I may just do that, soon as my relief gets here."

"Good. We'll look for you." The doors slid closed with a solid whump.

The trip that was usually over before Dawn noticed it had begun, seemed to take forever. When the shiny brass elevator doors finally slid open on the third floor, she found, to her chagrin, that she was on edge.

Imagine that. Must be because of the unfinished article.

She stepped into the hallway carrying the

covered pot as cautiously as possible. So far, so good. The quilted cozy she'd wrapped around it insulated her hands but the pan was both heavy and cumbersome, especially since she didn't want to hold it close to her body in case it sloshed.

Turning the knob and giving the office door a hard bump with her hip as she had her apartment door, she expected it to swing open. It didn't budge. It did, however, rattle on its hinges. She set the soup pot on the floor and crouched beside it so she could rummage through her shoulder bag for the key.

Suddenly, Tim jerked the door open.

Still hunkered down, Dawn was so startled she lost her balance and plopped into an awkward sitting position at his feet. Feeling a bit foolish but delighted she'd chosen to wear jeans rather than change into more suitable office attire, she tilted her head up and smiled. "Hi."

Tim was frowning. "What are you doing down there?"

"Right now? Sitting here."

"I can see that. What I meant was, it's Saturday. Why are you here at all?"

He held out his hand and she grasped it, letting him pull her to her feet. "I came to use the computer."

"You don't have one at home?"

"Nope. Never needed one till today. I get all the word processing I can stand during the week. When I'm off work I'd just as soon be out doing things, wouldn't you?" Dawn knew what his answer would be the minute she asked.

"No." He eyed the quilt-wrapped object on the floor. "What is that?"

"Our supper." She was brushing invisible dust off her clothing. "Would you mind? Be careful. It's hot."

Tim's scowl lines deepened. "What are you talking about? I didn't order any food."

"Of course you didn't. You rarely eat properly." As he bent to pick up the pot she sidled past him and led the way into the office.

Tim followed. "What is this stuff."

"Soup. I made it myself."

"You hauled a pot of hot soup all the way over here? You're crazy. You could have been burned."

"So far, so good," Dawn said brightly. She pointed. "Put it right there on the counter next to the coffeemaker. One of these days I'm going to have to spring for a Crock-Pot, I suppose. In the meantime, this works fine."

"It looks like you wrapped it in a sleeping bag."

She began untying the ribbons that had held the cozy in place. "Actually, I made this little quilt for taking hot food to church suppers. Of course, I can always warm food on the stove there if it cools too much. Since we don't have that option, we'd better dig in pretty soon. Either that or we'll have to nuke it."

"What?"

Bless his heart, he looks totally bumfuzzled, she thought with amusement. "I brought soup," she said as if explaining to a child. "You and I are going to eat it. Soon. Whether you like it or not. Understand?"

Tim had rolled up his shirtsleeves and shed his

usual silk tie before Dawn's arrival. Now, he folded his arms across his chest and struck a defensive pose. "We are, huh?"

"Yes, we are." She grinned at him. "You'll love it. I made it myself. From scratch."

"Why didn't you just open a can?"

"Where's the adventure in that?" she joked. "I didn't think to bring bowls so we'll have to spoon it out of coffee mugs."

"Suppose I'm not hungry?"

She eyed him mockingly and shook her head. "You're starving. I can hear your stomach growling all the way over here. It sounds worse than Beau's does when his supper's late."

"It does not." He placed the flat of one hand over his abdomen and gave her a doubtful look.

Dawn laughed. "Well, maybe not, but I've known you long enough to know that when you're working, you almost always skip meals."

"That's true."

"Besides, it would be impolite to refuse to taste it."

"I suppose it would." A lopsided smile began to spread across Tim's handsome face and his eyes twinkled. "Guess I'll be forced to eat some, won't I?"

"Guess so." She handed him a brimming mug and a spoon. "I hope it's not too hot for you. I used a few of my mama's favorite Cajun spices." She bowed her head over her own steaming cup and said, "Thank You, Father, for this good food and good company. Amen."

When she looked up, Tim was still standing there, mug in one hand, spoon in the other, staring at her.

"That was sure short and sweet," he said. "When my father says grace he usually covers everything from the sorry state of the world to the price of paper. When I was a kid we could count on our food getting cold before he was done."

Dawn chuckled warmly. "I figure God already knows all that other stuff so I just thank Him and get on with it. I've never been comfortable with too much formality, even in church."

"Interesting," Tim said. He blew gently on a spoonful of soup and tasted it. "Hey. This is good."

"And you're surprised? I should be offended."

"I didn't mean it that way. I can see now why you bother making this. Does it take a long time?"

"Yes. But some things, like good soup and true friendships, are better simmered slowly."

She smiled and made eye contact, suddenly far more self-assured than when she'd arrived. "And they're both definitely worth the wait."

Chapter Seven

Dawn had been so positive Tim would find fault with her efforts in writing about Stuart Meyers, she'd almost keeled over in a faint when he'd given the article high praise and had passed it on to Ed Bradshaw with orders to run it in the features section of the following week's special supplement to the paper. Moreover, judging by the nice letters and phone calls they'd received after it had appeared, readers of the *Davis Landing Dispatch* were equally pleased and impressed.

"I'm going to make this a weekly column," Tim told her, waving a folded copy for emphasis. "Even Bradshaw agrees, and he's usually the last one to accept change."

"Who are you going to get to write it?"

"I'm happy with the writer we already have."

Dawn's eyes widened. "Not *me?* Oh, no. You promised the job was only temporary."

"That was before I knew how good you were going to be at it," Tim said.

"I'm good at making soup, too. You said so yourself. But that doesn't mean I should open a restaurant."

He laughed. "True. Tell you what. Suppose I assign you and Felicity to alternate weeks? Would that be better?"

"Maybe. I had no idea how much work went into writing anything, let alone a person's whole life story. It's given me more respect for the business, that's for sure."

"Speaking of business," Tim said. "I have to put in an appearance at the yearly stockholder's get-together at Opryland in a few weeks." He grimaced. "I'd rather sit through a dozen regular board meetings than one of those black-tie dinners but I have no choice. For once, I wish Dad or Jeremy were back at the helm so they could go instead."

"I'm sorry." She was shuffling papers that needed filing and not looking at her boss as she offered standard words of commiseration. "Anything I can do to help?"

"As a matter of fact, yes."

Dawn's head snapped up. *"Yes?"* The question was followed by an unspoken *Uh-oh* and a shiver of trepidation.

"Yes. I thought the whole ordeal would be more bearable if you accompanied me this time."

"Me?"

"Sure. Why not? It'll do you good to get to know

some of the people you speak to on the phone. And I know there will be plenty of good food there so you won't have to bring your own like you do around this place."

She wasn't sure whether or not he was serious. "What about…" Racking her brain, she tried to remember the name of the romance du jour. "Gloria?"

"I'm not looking for a date," Tim said. "I want an intelligent companion who knows this business as well as I do." He smiled. "Or nearly as well."

"Nope. No way." Dawn was shaking her head so emphatically her blond hair swung against her cheeks. "Can't do it."

"Why not? The stockholders won't bite. And I'm not bad company, am I?"

"Of course not. It's not you. I…I don't have anything to wear to a formal dinner."

"What's wrong with what you have on right now?"

"Oh, sure. It'll be fine. I'll run right home and sew sequins all over the frilly ruffles on this blouse." The look of incredulity and condescension she sent Tim's way was enough to make him hesitate.

"Sarcasm? Right. Sarcasm. I get it." He rounded his desk and picked up the phone. Instead of dialing out, he pushed a button for interoffice communication and was immediately connected to his sister, downstairs in the *Nashville Living* office. "Heather? Tim. Listen, we have a fashion emergency in my office. Can you come up here for a second? Yes. Right now."

Dawn didn't know what his sister had said in reply but there was a definite look of smugness on Tim's face when he hung up and turned his attention back to her. "Okay. Problem solved. Our Makeover Maven is on her way."

"I don't need a makeover," Dawn protested.

"I don't think you do, either, but Heather's great with clothes, especially since she was made over herself. If you two put your heads together, I know you can come up with something suitable for you to wear to the dinner. I think she gets a lot of her clothes at Engel's Department Store."

"What part of 'no' don't you understand?"

"It's not in my vocabulary."

"You can say that again."

He began to do so. "It's not in—"

Dawn's "Arrrgh" was forceful enough to silence him but it did nothing to wipe the self-satisfied grin off his face.

"Okay," she finally said, pacing across the office and back. "Listen carefully. I can't buy anything at Engel's, period. I couldn't even afford one of their silk scarves. I know. I looked once. And I'm certainly not going to embarrass us both by wearing a dress I got at the local discount store. There's a world of difference. Believe me. Men might not be able to tell quality like that, but women can. I simply won't do it."

Tim had opened his mouth to answer when his younger sister breezed into the office. Heather's confidence had grown so much since her makeover it never ceased to amaze him. She had definitely come into her own and it was evident Tim was as proud of that blossoming confidence as she was.

"Heather! Boy, am I glad to see you," he blurted.

She scanned the office, looking confused. "I thought you said there was an emergency."

"There is." Tim palmed a credit card and Dawn saw him pass it to his sister as he headed for the door. "Use that. I've got to run."

Dawn made a face and called after him, "Chicken!"

When she turned her attention back to Heather, the look of astonishment on the poor girl's face was so funny she couldn't help smiling. "It's a long story."

"Take as long as you need," Heather said. "Anything that has my oh-so-perfect big brother this flustered has to be worth hanging around long enough to hear." She perched a slim hip on the edge of Dawn's desk. "Okay, give. And don't leave anything out. I want to hear all the juicy details."

Tim lay low until he saw both women leaving the building. Together. Smiling and chatting. That was a good sign. It also meant he could return to his office without encountering either of them or having to explain what urgent, imaginary errand had taken him away in the first place.

Women. Can't live with 'em, can't live with 'em, he rephrased inaccurately, much to his own amusement. Boy, was *that* the truth. It seemed as though the more he tried to relate to Dawn, to understand her, the more trouble he got himself into.

A lot of their conflict had to do with finances, he assumed, given her negative reaction to his suggestion that she accompany him to the dinner at Opryland. Who would have guessed she'd think she had to have different clothes? All the other women he knew, his mother and sisters included, had everything they needed in their own closets at home. Of course, that didn't mean they didn't buy a new outfit at the drop of a credit card. Dawn probably could have worn a dress she already owned, too, if she hadn't been so stubborn. He'd never seen her in anything that didn't make her look attractive—including the jeans she'd worn the night she'd shown up with the pot of soup.

That kind of personal reflection brought him up short. Since when was it appropriate for a man to think of his executive assistant as a beautiful woman?

When she was, he answered easily. Dawn Leroux was beautiful—inside and out. The way she cared about others was part of her charm. And it was what made her so good at her job, whether she was working at Hamilton Media or volunteering in the community. Her pure heart shone through and colored whatever she did.

That was why he'd asked her to go to the stockholders' gala with him, Tim told himself. It was a perfectly plausible reason. He did want an intelligent companion and he valued Dawn's opinions.

Therefore, what could be more logical than to include her in the after-hours dinner meeting?

Riding the elevator back to the third floor he let his mind wander. What kind of dress would she choose with Heather at her side? he wondered. Maybe he should have told his sister how good Dawn looked in blue. It brought out the summer sky in her eyes and made her skin glow with just the right amount of warmth. And that long, blond hair of hers! Ada Smith had been right on target when she'd remarked on its beauty.

The elevator doors slid open. Jarred from his reverie, Tim started to exit as his sister, Amy, stepped on.

"Hi. I was just on my way up to see you," Amy said with a smile. "But if you're getting off here, I'll wait."

Tim wasn't about to admit he'd been so caught up in his daydreaming about Dawn he hadn't even realized what floor he'd stopped on. Instead, he stepped back and motioned for his eldest sister to join him. "No problem. Come on. We can talk in my office."

"Oh? Is Heather gone?"

"I just saw her leave," Tim said with a suppressed sigh. "Hopefully, she and my assistant will be out all afternoon."

"That was what I wanted to talk to you about," Amy said.

Raising an eyebrow, Tim crossed his arms over his chest and nodded. "Yeah. I figured you'd want to know what was going on as soon as the news hit the office grapevine. It started out as a simple idea, honest. Somehow, things got out of hand."

The elevator had hummed its way to the third floor and the doors were sliding open. "How simple?" Amy asked.

Tim blocked the door with his hand so it wouldn't close too soon. "All I did was ask Dawn to go to the stockholders' dinner with me. The next thing I knew, I was sending Heather to Engel's with my assistant and my gold card."

"That makes perfect sense to me," Amy said with a knowing smile. "It's black-tie. Dawn probably needed something nice to wear."

"That's what she said. I don't get it. I mean, I understand her wanting a new dress for the occasion. All the women I know act like that. I just can't see what the big deal is if she has to wear what she already has in her closet. She always looks great to me."

"Oooooh," his sister drawled. "Have you told her that?"

"I don't know. I suppose I have. Why?"

Amy merely shook her head and stared at him. "For a savvy executive in charge of a company the size of this one, you sure can be dense sometimes."

"I don't want to spend Tim's money," Dawn insisted, peeking at her companion between the dresses on the rack at Engel's. "If I have to do this, I'll pay for it myself."

Heather was adamant. "Nonsense. Tim said this was for a business dinner and he's as good as commanding you to go, so he should have to pay. It's no different than it would be if somebody like Ed Bradshaw had to rent a tux."

"I hadn't thought of it that way."

"Well, start to," Heather said with a smile. "I'd offer to lend you something new of mine if we had the same basic coloring but I don't think I have anything appropriate that would do you justice." She held up a slim, shimmering, teal-blue sheath with a handkerchief hemline. "How about this one? It's perfect with your hair and eyes."

"It is pretty fabric." Dawn lifted the sleeve, read the attached price tag and dropped it as though it had burned her fingers. "No way!"

"Oh, come on. It'll serve Tim right if we charge some expensive stuff. Besides, it's against the Code of Women to refuse to spend a man's money when he offers."

"What Code of Women?"

Heather giggled. "I just made that up. If there isn't a code like that, there should be. Think about it. Suppose Tim told you he wanted a hundred copies of a fancy, full-color brochure and the copy machine at the office was broken? Would you write them all out in longhand and then color them with crayons? Or would you go find the equipment to do the job right?"

Dawn got her point but made a wry face anyway. "Okay. I'll try on a few things. But let's be sensible about this. I don't want to bankrupt the poor man."

Heather just rolled her eyes.

"Well, I don't," Dawn insisted. "It's not right to take advantage of this situation, even if Tim did bring it on himself."

"Fine. Whatever," Heather said as she grabbed several more dresses off the rack and slung them over her arm. "Come on. Let's try these on you for starters. I don't want to bother looking for shoes or other accessories till we see what basic color scheme we're dealing with."

Dawn was lagging behind. "Shoes? Accessories? Wait a minute. Who said anything about all that?"

"I did. You don't expect me to abdicate my duty to *Nashville Living,* do you? Their new Makeover Maven can't turn out a half-complete Cinderella job. I have a reputation to protect. Can't be slipshod. How would it look to my boss?"

"Your sister Amy is your boss."

"Right. And Tim is everybody's boss these days, even Amy's. When he says 'Jump,' we all ask, 'How high?'"

Sighing, Dawn quit arguing and followed Heather to the dressing rooms. This day had certainly been eventful. And it was far from over. If Tim's sister had her way, his credit card would be in meltdown in a few hours. The question was, how could Dawn rationalize accepting that kind of expensive treatment, even at Heather's insistence? It didn't seem right. Or proper. Or even smart. Yet she couldn't see a graceful way out of the situation.

The current state of affairs wasn't merely a challenge to her sensibilities, she realized with a jolt. It was a test of her faith. If she truly believed God's hand was guiding every aspect of her life—which she did—how could she question the recent turn of events without also doubting her Heavenly Father's wisdom? How, indeed?

Gown. Shoes. Purse. Dawn's head was swimming by the time she and Heather had finished shopping. She'd put her foot down when Tim's sister had suggested buying jewelry, agreeing to borrow something, instead. Unfortunately, that choice had proven at least as troubling as the purchases they'd made because Heather still lived at home with her parents.

Dawn was already in awe of the whole family so she wasn't thrilled with Heather's suggestion they drop in at the Hamilton mansion to look at jewelry on their way back to the office. With Heather driving, however, she had no choice but to go along with the idea.

The Hamiltons didn't call their residence a mansion, of course. They had too much class for that. To them it was merely their ancestral home; an enormous, old, redbrick, Greek Revival–style house at the very outer edge of north Davis Landing. Dawn had seen it from the outside many times and had tried to imagine what the interior might look like but she wasn't prepared for the real thing.

Heather led her through the heavy, leaded-glass front door and into the foyer. "Here we are. Home sweet home."

Dawn didn't know what to say. "It's…it's big."

The other woman's laugh echoed in the cavernous entryway. "It sure didn't seem big when we were kids. We were always stumbling over each other."

"That's hard to believe." Dawn had taken a few tentative steps on the highly polished hardwood floor and was staring up at the colored light reflecting off the crystal prisms in the chandelier. "Wow."

Heather gestured toward a sweeping central staircase. "My room's on the third floor. Most of the good jewelry's kept down here, in Dad's safe in the library. We'll cut through the parlor so you can see grandmother's grand piano. Mom made all of us take lessons when we were kids. Boy, did my brothers hate it. Do you play?"

"No." Dawn shook her head and followed, trying to remember to keep her mouth closed instead of gaping at the opulence. Feeling totally out of place, she gave a nervous little laugh when an amusing thought crossed her mind.

"What's so funny?" Heather asked pleasantly.

"Oh, nothing. I was just thinking how I'd hate to have to dust all these ornate antiques."

"Vera Mae takes care of that," Heather said. "She's been our cook and housekeeper for as long as I can remember. When I was little, I used to think she was older than dirt."

Dawn suppressed another laugh. "What, no butler?"

"Not anymore. There was a butler's pantry off the kitchen. It's been obsolete since one of the remodels where they opened up the smaller areas and combined the formal and informal dining rooms. I keep telling Mom she needs more help, especially lately, but she refuses to hire anyone besides Vera Mae. Of course, there is a service that keeps up the lawn and gardens."

"Of course." Dawn didn't have the heart to tell Heather she'd been joking when she'd mentioned a butler. She couldn't even imagine living in a house that was more like a museum than a home. And the notion of having even one servant boggled her mind. There were larger, more modern dwellings in the newer areas of Davis Landing, but she doubted there were any that could rival the Hamilton place for sheer lavishness.

Heather led her into a room that had more bookshelves lining the walls than Betty's Bakeshoppe and Bookstore. In one corner, two matching high-backed chairs were grouped around a carved mahogany side table. A glass-shaded floor lamp of brass, with an inlaid alabaster base, arched over the table like a graceful, long-necked whooping crane about to snap up a hapless fish. As if a decorator had read her thoughts beforehand, a lifelike bisque figure of a wading bird stood poised on the side table.

Didn't these people own anything that wasn't old and fragile? Dawn was almost afraid to breathe.

She sure hoped she didn't have to sneeze while she was in this room because everything except the massive desk and the books looked decidedly breakable.

"We'll take a peek at the particular necklace I have in mind and then decide," Heather said, going directly to an eye-level shelf and removing a set of leather-bound tomes to gain access to a small safe with a combination dial. "Mom has lots of beautiful things."

"Hold it." Dawn put on the brakes. "I thought you were going to loan me something of yours."

Heather laughed. "I don't wear diamonds. It's not my style. But Mom has oodles of pretty pieces. There's one in particular that I'm sure would be perfect with the neckline of your new dress."

"I can't borrow your mother's jewels! What if I lost one?" She swallowed hard. "What if I lost a whole necklace? What if I got mugged or something?"

"Oh, stop worrying. Tim will take good care of you." Heather had the safe open and was removing a dark velvet box. "Here." She opened it and displayed its contents. "What do you think of this one?"

Dawn gasped. The silver filigreed necklace and matching earrings were delicately crafted. Just enough diamond sparkle had been incorporated to set off the artistic design without making the pieces gaudy. Her hand trembled as she reached to gently touch the outer edge of the velvet box. "How beautiful!"

"I think so, too. And Mom rarely wears the set. Seems like a shame to have it sitting in the dark in this old safe, doesn't it? I'll ask her to be sure, but I'm positive she'll be delighted to lend it to you for one evening. Can't you picture it with the scooped neckline of that beautiful blue dress we bought? Talk about gorgeous!"

Dawn felt as if she were a helium-filled balloon that had suddenly sprung a leak. "I can't wear that. Really, I can't."

Heather laid a hand lightly on Dawn's shoulder. "You can and you will. It's about time somebody knocked my stuffy brother's socks off and I think you're just the one who can do it."

"I don't want to knock anybody's socks off," Dawn lamented. "I want to go back to the office and pretend all this never happened."

"Well, I can take you back to work, but I can't do anything about canceling out the afternoon," Heather said with obvious glee. "I wish I could be a little fly on the wall so I could hide and see Tim's face when he gets his first look at you in that dress, though."

Dawn sighed and shook her head. "Speaking of seeing things, I hope he decides he loves the outfit before he sees the bill for it and faints dead away."

Chapter Eight

Opryland was a Nashville institution, one that Dawn had heard plenty about but hadn't visited. She'd cited various excuses for not having sampled any of the attractions at the resort and convention center complex but the main reason was monetary.

Though she was living comfortably while still sending money to her parents, she hadn't budgeted anything extra for entertaining herself. She hadn't needed to. Beau kept her amused at home and Northside Community Church, with its diverse members and outreach programs, had become her emotional and physical escape.

There was always plenty going on around the church, even during the week, and she enjoyed the aura of peace and love that always enveloped her and made her feel at home there. That was one of the reasons she'd agreed to teach Sunday school on a regular basis and why she didn't mind spending that whole evening sprucing up the Sunday school rooms for the six- to eight-year-olds with her friend and fellow teacher, Gabi.

Thanks to Northside and the example of its beloved pastor, David Abernathy, Dawn was always adding to her growing list of friends. Besides Gabi and Gabi's young daughters, Veronica, Roni for short, who was ten going on twenty-five, and Talia, a lovable eight-year-old, she'd also grown close to Felicity Simmons from the *Dispatch* and Stella Barton, who worked at the hospital with Gabi.

Recently, she'd heard quite a lot about Melissa Hamilton, too, mainly when the church's young adults group met. Now that the youngest Hamilton had run off to who-knows-where, someone was always asking for prayer on her behalf. From the tone of the requests, Dawn had concluded Melissa's prolonged absence was of concern, particularly to her family and those who knew her best.

She'd contemplated asking Tim if he'd had any word from his baby sister, then thought better of it. If she wanted answers to personal questions, it would be much wiser to ask Heather. Dawn liked her, really liked her, especially after they'd shared the shopping experience, even if Heather was a rich kid from the right side of the tracks.

"I *like* my side of the tracks," Dawn mumbled.

Across the otherwise empty Sunday school room, Gabi perked up. "What did you say?"

"Nothing." Dawn shrugged. "I was just thinking out loud."

"Sounds serious. Anything I can do to help?"

"Oooh. Better be careful when you say that. Last time I did, Tim roped me into going to that fancy dinner that's coming up."

"It's next Saturday night, isn't it?"

Dawn made a face at Gabi. "Yeah. Whoopie."

"Hey, don't complain. You got a new dress out of the deal. It's *muy bonita,* as my *mamacita* would say."

"It is pretty. I don't mean to sound ungrateful but it's such a waste. Where in the world am I ever going to wear a dress like that again?"

"Maybe Tim will decide he wants to take you out more than once."

"Dreamer."

"Well, maybe he will. You never know. You said he's mellowed lately."

Dawn's eyebrows arched and she nodded. "That's true." The hint of a smile quirked one corner of her mouth. "I can just picture it. He'll be in a different shirt and tie every time he picks me up and I'll be wearing that same blue dress, over and over again."

"At least he'll get his money's worth," Gabi teased.

"Not unless I live in that dress for the rest of my life—and then some. I can't believe anybody pays that much for clothes. And the shoes were nearly as bad. I can't remember exactly what they were called. Their name sounded like an Italian opera singer crossed with a Russian cobbler."

Gabi giggled. "I think I've heard of that brand. Very trendy. Are they comfortable?"

"I don't know. I guess so. I'm going to be too nervous to notice my feet, anyway." She paced to the bulletin board and busied herself pinning up illustrations of the upcoming month's Sunday school lessons.

"You'll do fine," her friend assured her. "How are you going to wear your hair?"

Dawn frowned. "My hair?"

"Sure. Are you going with an up-do or leaving it loose, like always?"

Laying aside the pushpins she'd been using at the bulletin board, she raked the fingers of both hands through her tresses and lifted them high in the back. "You mean up? Like this? Why would I do that?"

"To look more sophisticated."

"Phooey. I'm not going to fool anybody into thinking I actually belong at that stockholders dinner no matter what I do," Dawn countered, shaking out her hair and resuming the decorating task. "Why should I try?"

"It's not about trying to fool anyone," Gabi argued. "It's called putting your best foot forward." She tittered. "After all, you'll be wearing expensive shoes on those feet."

"Very funny."

"I could do your hair for you. I used to put my own up all the time when Octavio was alive. Now, I don't take the time to fuss with it. Too much bother."

Dawn shrugged noncommittally. "You can fiddle with my hair if you want to. I hadn't actually considered doing anything different with it but it might make me feel more elegant. I need all the help I can get at this point."

"You'll do fine. Don't put yourself down," Gabi said. "Tim obviously feels comfortable taking you or he wouldn't have asked you to go in the first place."

"That's true. But—"

"No buts. It's settled. I'll be over Saturday morning to do your hair. We can make it a girls-only party and unwind together."

"Speaking of girls," Dawn said. "What about Talia and Roni? Want to bring them, too? We can all pig out on pizza. My treat."

"Sounds wonderful. I'll tell them we're getting Cinderella ready to go to the ball with her prince. Roni will probably roll her eyes and look at me like I'm crazy but Talia will love the idea. Besides, they love to come over and play with your dog."

Dawn nodded. Her mind was already spinning off on a detour triggered by Gabi's mention of a prince. She'd never seen Tim Hamilton in a tuxedo but she could imagine how he'd look. *Princely* pretty much summed it up.

Oh, Father, she thought, *help me. I don't know why You've put me in this position but I don't feel adequate to cope with it. Please, please, stay with me. I can't do it without You.*

That short prayer was so honest it opened her eyes to the truth she'd been overlooking. She wasn't in this alone. She never had been. Trusting God for the easy things in life was usually relatively painless. The true test of her faith was trusting

Him—*really* trusting Him—during difficult times and in confusing circumstances.

Dawn smiled, realizing that the answer to her prayer had been within her all along. Her focus was wrong. Instead of worrying about what other people thought of her she needed to keep her eyes on Jesus and live the way He'd taught. Doing that would bring everything else into line, no matter what occurred.

"'I can do all things through Christ who strengthens me,'" she quoted, looking over at Gabi for affirmation.

The pretty Latina nodded. "Right on, sister. Now you've got it. You're going to have a wonderful time."

Having Gabi and the girls keep her company in her small apartment all afternoon that fateful Saturday helped Dawn stay distracted. And watching the girls babying Beau had given them all plenty to laugh about. Once the others left, however, the butterflies in Dawn's stomach started to flap their little imaginary wings something awful.

Dressed in the shimmering blue dress, she pivoted in front of the full-length mirror on the back of her bathroom door and stared at her image, barely recognizing the slim, sophisticated woman looking back at her. Where had the real Dawn Leroux gone? That certainly wasn't her in the mirror! That woman was too beautiful. Too elegant. And too unsteady in such high-heeled shoes, she added with concern. Losing her balance in those stupid shoes and taking a spill in front of all the stockholders would make a lasting impression on them, all right.

She lightly patted the upswept hairdo Gabi had created. It was becoming, but it further emphasized the contrast she felt between who she really was and who she was pretending to be. That bothered her. She felt she should be comfortable as herself, not trying to impress people by changing her appearance.

About to pull the pins and release her hair to fall around her face and over her shoulders as it usually did, Dawn was startled by a knock.

Beau was worn out from his afternoon efforts at entertaining Gabi's girls but he nevertheless raised his head and managed one halfhearted "woof."

"It's okay, boy," Dawn said. Giving him the corresponding hand signals she said, "Down. Stay."

He yawned and looked relieved, closed his eyes and stretched out on his side, clearly ready to resume his interrupted nap.

Dawn's glance darted to the kitchen clock. Who could be at the door? Tim wasn't due for another hour. Maybe Gabi had forgotten something and had returned for it.

She called, "Coming," and made her way across the living room, careful to balance in the new shoes.

Smiling, she opened the door. "Hi! Did you… "

It was Tim! Dawn was speechless. There he stood, in all his tuxedoed perfection, not a hair out of place and more handsome than ever. In one hand he held the velvet jewelry box Heather had shown her at the Hamilton house.

She boldly looked him up and down without realizing she was doing it. When her gaze rose to rest on his face she was startled to see an expression that revealed more than mere surprise. Apparently Heather had gotten her wish. The man was obviously shocked all the way to his socks! Well, no wonder. She was pretty surprised at the transformation she saw in her mirror, too.

Turning from side to side to display the shimmering dress Dawn asked, "How do you like it?"

"It's…it's—" Tim seemed at a loss for words. Finally he settled on "—amazing."

"Thank you." She stepped aside. "My friend Gabi and I had a pizza party this afternoon while she did my hair so I'm afraid the place is a little messy, but you're welcome to come in for a minute if you'd like."

The shake of Tim's head was barely discernible. He peered past her to assess the dozing mastiff. "No, thanks. Looks like Beau wouldn't mind but it still wouldn't look right to your neighbors." He handed her the velvet box. "Mom sent this. Heather said you knew all about it."

"Yes. Thank you." Accepting the small, flat jewelry box, Dawn noticed that her hand was shaking. "I don't mind telling you, wearing this scares me to death. But your sister wouldn't take no for an answer."

She left the door standing open as she lifted the hinged lid of the box and once again saw the magnificent necklace. "Oh, my. It's even more beautiful than I remembered."

"Much more beautiful," Tim said quietly.

His voice was low and a little hoarse-sounding, leading Dawn to glance back at him. Judging by the direct way his gaze met hers, she was tempted to imagine he was referring to her rather than to the diamond necklace.

She lifted it gingerly. "I don't know if I can fasten this properly. I wouldn't want it to fall off and get lost." She looked pleadingly at Tim and held the necklace out to him. "Would you do it for me?"

He took it. "Turn around."

As she did so, he closed the distance between them and Dawn sensed his overpowering presence. She'd always been aware of Tim's charisma but she'd never before noticed his nearness affecting her this much. He wasn't touching her, yet she felt as if he'd put his arms around her and pulled her into his embrace.

The necklace brushed against her skin and settled at her throat. She placed the fingertips of one hand over it. Her pulse was racing so rapidly she was certain Tim could see the beats jumping below her jawline.

In moments he'd fastened the necklace and stepped back. He cleared his throat. "Can you manage the earrings?"

"I think so." Dawn laid the box on an end table so she'd have both hands free. Her ears were pierced and the posts were screw-on so she wasn't as worried about losing the delicate drop earrings.

When she finished she looked to Tim. "There. How's that? I hope it's not too much."

"It's perfect." His voice was deep, his tone sensitive. "You're perfect." At that, he began to smile. "I hope I get to spend a little time with you after all the other men get through fawning over you."

"Hah. Nobody ever fawns over me," she said, "except maybe Beau." The weary dog opened one eye and thumped his tail against the floor at the mention of his name.

"Well, they will tonight. I guarantee it. Are you ready to go?"

"Yes, but… Aren't we awfully early?"

"You said you'd never been to Opryland before so I thought we'd walk around the grounds first. They have acres of gardens with waterfalls and even a river, all under a glass atrium. I think you'll enjoy it."

Dawn hesitated. "Walk?"

"We could ride the riverboat if you'd rather."

"It's just these shoes," Dawn explained. "Heather insisted on them but I'm not used to such high heels. I'm not sure how good they'll be for taking a leisurely stroll."

"I wouldn't care if you went barefoot," Tim said, smiling. "Come on. Let's get out of here before I give in to hunger and beg a piece of your leftover pizza. It smells delicious."

"It was. But I'm afraid you're too late. Gabi and the girls were here all afternoon and they saw to it that Beau got all the scraps. There's nothing left but the cardboard box."

"Then I guess I'll have to wait for the fancy cuisine at the Ristorante Volare. It's always been very good."

Dawn picked up the clutch Heather had chosen to match her outfit, made sure she had her key and joined Tim at the door. "Okay. Guess I'm as ready as I'll ever be."

"Do you have a wrap? It might be chilly later."

"Nope, no wrap. I told your sister I'd rather freeze to death tonight than spend one more penny of your money."

Laughing softly, he offered her his arm. "In that case, Ms. Leroux, to show my appreciation, I promise I'll give you my jacket to wear if you need it."

Although she said, "It's a deal," in her heart-of-hearts she was hoping and praying his sacrifice of his own comfort wouldn't be necessary. Her senses were already so on edge she was afraid she'd self-destruct if she actually donned a coat that was still warm with Tim's body heat and smelling of his after-shave.

Her high-fashion shoes weren't the only un-steadying thing she was dealing with tonight. Ever since Tim had arrived at her door she'd felt as though her whole world was wobbling out of kilter and that feeling was getting stronger by the minute. When Gabi had warned her to be careful about swimming with sharks, she'd forgotten to mention how handsome and charming those sharks could be.

The evening she and Tim had spent delivering meals to Stuart and Ada and the others had been nothing compared to the challenges she was about to encounter. This was a whole new universe for a simple girl from the bayous. Now that she thought about it, the possibility of falling on her face had a lot less to do with her shoes than it did with her sheltered upbringing.

Then again, Dawn reminded herself, she wasn't ashamed of her background and she intended to make no apologies for it. As a child, she'd played school by dressing up one of her father's old hound dogs and pretending it was her only pupil while she'd taught a make-believe class.

Attending this gala with Tim had a lot of similarities to that child's pastime. When her game was over and the clothing removed, the old dog had still been a dog. When this evening ended and she took off the diamonds and other finery, she'd still be Tim's capable executive assistant. Nothing more. Nothing less.

She didn't lament the truth of her conclusion. It was simply how things were. How they should be. She didn't fit into his high-powered world any better than he'd fit in at one of her parents' outdoor crawdad boils down in Louisiana, with its ethnic food and uniquely Cajun zydeco music. The memory of her happy childhood made her smile.

Tim paused to open the car door for her. "Is something funny?" he asked.

"No. I was just remembering how much fun it was when I was little and life was so easy and uncomplicated."

He looked puzzled as he replied, "That sounds odd to me. I can't recall a time when I didn't take everything seriously."

Dawn averted her eyes so he wouldn't be able to discern her innermost thoughts. She didn't want him to know she thought that was the saddest confession she'd ever heard.

Chapter Nine

Passing through Nashville to Opryland would have taken longer if they hadn't been making the trip on a Saturday evening. Still, the traffic on Highway 65 was ample.

"I play golf over there," Tim said, pointing as they passed a beautifully manicured course. He'd been trying unsuccessfully to get Dawn involved in a conversation ever since they'd left Hickory Mills. For a person who usually had an opinion about everything, she was being far too quiet to suit him.

She merely nodded.

"Have you ever played?"

"Golf?" She shook her head. "No."

"Would you like to learn?" Her raised eyebrow prodded him to add, "It's good for you. I mean, if you're interested in healthy hobbies you can get great exercise walking the golf course."

"Unless you ride in one of those little electric carts," she said. "Do you?"

"Well, sometimes. But it still gets me out in the sun and fresh air."

"True. I suppose it is better than living at your desk 24-7. Did you go to the office today?"

"Yes. Why?"

"I just wondered."

Judging by her tone and the look on her face, Dawn didn't think much of his work ethic. Tim couldn't understand why she had such a problem with it. She always put in a full day's work without shirking so why should she begrudge him the same kind of dedication?

He decided to ask. "Why am I getting the impression you think I work too much?"

"Because you do," she answered. "You don't seem to know how to relax and have fun."

"I'm relaxing right now," Tim said. "This is enjoyable, isn't it?" He was sorry the minute the words were out of his mouth. Dawn's arching eyebrow and wide-eyed, silent response told him she definitely disagreed.

He persevered. "So it's a stockholder's meeting. So what? That doesn't mean we can't have a little fun, too. We're certainly dressed for it."

That brought a cynical laugh from his companion. "Hah! I'm so uptight I almost hate to breathe for fear something will snap and I'll self-destruct." She paused. "Don't get me wrong, Tim. I do appreciate your thoughtfulness in paying for this outfit.

Really, I do. But my idea of having fun requires a lot less finery and a lot more spontaneity."

"I can be spontaneous in a tuxedo."

"Maybe you can, but I'm afraid to move for fear my dress will rip or my shoes will dump me in a ditch or my hair will fall down or something equally embarrassing."

"I did wonder about that," he said. "Why did you put your hair up like that? It makes you look—"

Her head snapped around. "What? It makes me look what? Sophisticated?"

"Well…" A blush threatened and he forced himself to subdue it by thinking logically. "I was going to say more formal. You usually look so ap-proachable it's kind of off-putting."

Instead of the huff he'd expected, he heard Dawn sigh, then saw her reach up and begin to remove pins until her hair fell free to swing against her shoulders.

"Wait! I didn't mean you had to take it down," Tim said.

"I know." Her voice sounded softer, as if she were relieved to have reclaimed a portion of her normal persona. She was rummaging around in her small handbag. "Uh-oh. I forgot to bring a hair-brush."

Tim smiled at her wide-eyed artlessness. "We can fix that. I'll stop and buy you one. Just tell me where."

"Any drugstore will be fine. I'm not fussy."

It pleased him to have finally found something

he could get for her that didn't make her scowl. He took the nearest off-ramp and pulled into the parking lot of a strip mall.

"You coming?" he asked.

"Not dressed like this," Dawn answered. "Just pick up a little brush I can stick into this purse. Nothing fancy, okay?"

"Sure. Be right back."

Tim left her and headed for the store. He'd never shopped for anything like a woman's hairbrush before but he figured it couldn't be that hard. If he was capable of heading a media empire, he could certainly manage to locate one suitable item in a discount drug store.

The overhead signs directed him to the right area. After he found the display of hair accessories, however, he just stood there and stared. Though he had a dozen choices, none of them seemed to be the kind of quality merchandise he preferred.

He checked his watch. There wasn't enough time to return to Engel's or look for a similar upscale department store in Nashville, so he decided to settle for what was at hand.

Rather than try to choose one brush from among the many, he simply gathered up everything he thought might please Dawn and purchased the whole lot. Returning to the car he handed her the bulging plastic sack.

Her mouth dropped open. "What's all this?"

"A hairbrush. Pick the one you want and toss the rest into the backseat."

"You bought them *all?*" She was staring into the open top of the sack.

"No. Just the littler ones. I wanted to be sure you had what you needed."

Instead of the thanks he'd expected, Tim saw her lips press into a thin line. Finally, she took a brush from the bag and opened the plastic bubble covering it.

Admiring her as she brushed her silky hair, he was feeling a sense of accomplishment until she said, "You have too much money, Mr. Hamilton. Way, way too much money."

Dawn couldn't help being awed by the entrance to Opryland. A wide, circular drive led to a massive, airy building whose columns and porticos reminded her of the Hamilton house, only on a much grander scale. A uniformed doorman opened her door and greeted her like royalty.

Tim handed his car keys to the parking valet in exchange for a claim check, then joined her and offered his arm. "Shall we?"

"I guess it's too late to change my mind now, huh?" The crestfallen look on his face spurred her to add, "Just kidding," and loop her hand through the crook of his elbow as they climbed the stairs together.

Inside, the vastness and splendor of the lobby took her breath away. Rich, red brocade carpet covered the floor. An irregularly shaped ceiling of varnished wood with white beams rose to a peak like a giant teepee above a crystal and brass chandelier that had to be fifteen or twenty feet across. Potted ferns as big as trees softened the decor and a sweeping staircase rose, then divided, flanking the lower lobby with open balconies.

Dawn faltered. "Oh, my!"

"I thought you'd be impressed," Tim said. "Wait till you see the atrium. I'm not much into plants but whoever keeps the grounds must be a master gardener."

He led her through the lobby and out the opposite side.

Dawn breathed a quiet, "Wow." She'd imagined a greenhouse stretched over a garden but never anything of this magnitude and beauty. In keeping with nature's flowing design, there wasn't a straight line in the place. An indoor river, complete with sightseeing boats, curved around islands of greenery and multistoried buildings she assumed must house shops or restaurants. Above, steel beams supported a roof that was so high it arched over full-size trees the likes of those growing in Sugar Tree Park.

Tim guided her along a wide promenade. "I thought you'd be pleasantly surprised."

"That's an understatement. Umm. Smell the honeysuckle? I'm amazed it's still in bloom this late in the fall." She paused and cocked her head, listening. "Is that running water?"

"Uh-huh. There's a waterfall on the other side of these buildings. I think that's where they have the laser light shows after dark."

She grinned. "I hate to keep repeating myself but *wow!* This place is unbelievable."

They paused at the metal railing of an elevated walkway. "This is the skywalk," Tim said. "Behind us is the hotel and over there is the terrace of the Ristorante Volare where we'll be having dinner."

"You would have to remind me."

She was still holding on to his arm and he covered her hand with his. "Are you teasing, or does being here really upset you that much?"

"A little of both, I guess," she said with an audible sigh. "I'm not used to your lifestyle. I just hope I don't embarrass you, that's all."

"Never," Tim said.

Dawn sensed his sincerity even as an inner voice warned against taking him too seriously. Tim, like the rest of the Hamilton men, was a business-first kind of guy. If he thought her presence would be an asset, he'd include her. If he thought she might prove a detriment to his career, he'd dump her like a load of trash.

The earthy analogy did nothing to comfort her. Growing up near the New Orleans waterfront, she'd heard more than one person refer to her friends and family as trash. As an adult, she knew how unfair that label was, yet old hurts that deep were hard to forget. Yes, God loved her. Yes, God accepted her, no matter what. But that didn't mean everyone else felt the same way. If Tim had actually seen her humble origins, he might be less inclined to include her in anything, let alone dinner with his board and stockholders.

Then again, Dawn thought, smiling, if her daddy thought Tim wasn't giving his little girl the proper respect, he just might hurl him off a pier into the bay and ask questions later. The image of the oh-so-perfect Tim Hamilton, dressed like a penguin and bobbing like a cork in the ocean, amused her greatly.

Tim bent to study her face. "That's better. I thought I was never going to get you to smile."

She blushed. Good thing he didn't suspect what she'd found to smile about!

The banquet room at the restaurant was so crowded Dawn ceased to worry about losing her balance. Even if she did totter, she reasoned, she couldn't fall all the way down. These people were packed together so closely it would be impossible to reach the floor.

Tim had been shaking hands and introducing her to so many attendees that their names and faces had become a blur. The only one who really stood out was Richard McNeil, an attorney she'd met more than once at the Hamilton Media offices. He was a big man, heavier than Tim and a little taller, with the same dark hair but lighter-colored eyes. He shook her hand, then raised his empty glass. "I need a refill. What are you two drinking?"

"Sparkling water with a twist," Tim said. He looked to Dawn. "You?"

"That sounds fine."

Richard excused himself with a nod and turned

to elbow his way through the crowd to the bar. She was glad Tim had spoken up and ordered something nonalcoholic. It was comforting to know she wasn't going to have to insist on driving home because he'd been drinking. Most of the other revelers seemed to be doing just that, apparently taking advantage of the special wines offered at the open bar.

The lawyer returned carrying three glasses dressed with thin slices of lime. "Here you go." He smiled at Dawn and handed her one first. "How's the boss been treating you?"

"I can't complain," she said pleasantly.

Richard arched an eyebrow and grinned. "Would it do you any good?"

"Nope." His banter was relaxing her. He turned to Tim. "How about you? We haven't seen you around much lately."

"I'm not slaving as hard as I used to. I've decided that life's too short."

"Amen to that." She raised her glass and clinked it against his.

Richard lowered his voice to continue. "Look at Wallace, for instance. He didn't take the time to stop and smell the roses and now he may not get another chance."

"I hope he does," Dawn said sincerely.

"So do I. When God gives us a second chance, I think we appreciate it more, don't you?" Richard queried.

"I suppose so."

Tim waved and called a greeting to someone across the room before turning his attention back to Dawn and McNeil. "Say, Richard, did Dawn tell you she's writing for the paper, now? I've got her doing a regular human interest feature."

"Really? That's nice."

"Yes," Dawn said, "I've discovered—"

"Hey, I forgot to tell you," the attorney said, concentrating on Tim, "I got one of those new titanium drivers we talked about. It has a 450cc adjustable head and a graphite shaft with a low kick point."

"No kidding? How does it play?"

"Great. I've almost gotten rid of my slice."

Dawn listened quietly. They were apparently talking about golf. She sipped her water and bided her time rather than try to comment and show her ignorance. The urge to change the subject to a topic with which she was familiar was strong. She resisted. Two more men had now joined Tim and Richard's conversation and she was fairly certain none of them would be interested in swapping stories of crawdad fishing or dodging alligators in a mangrove swamp.

Then again, she thought, smiling sweetly and nodding unspoken greetings as others passed, one of those fancy golf clubs they were bragging about might be just the thing for beating off a nasty-tempered, hungry gator!

The image that idea brought to mind almost made her forget herself and laugh out loud.

She was still enjoying the picture of wading into

a swamp, dressed as she currently was and armed with a shiny new golf club for self-defense, when dinner was announced.

Tim led her to the head table and held her chair.

"You didn't tell me we were going to be on display," she whispered as she took her seat.

"I never gave it much thought," he said. "Dad always sat up here with the board. It didn't occur to me you might not know that."

"Are there any other things you failed to mention?" she asked aside.

"I don't think so. But feel free to kick me under the table if something else bothers you."

"Can't," Dawn said, stifling a nervous giggle. "There are no toes in these shoes and I don't want to hurt myself."

"Whew! That's a relief. I was beginning to worry."

"Sure, you were."

The crowd slowly found places at the other tables and quieted. Dawn watched Tim out of the corner of her eye as he stood and addressed the assemblage, welcoming them to the meeting on behalf of his ailing father and the firm. He displayed an air of command and self-assurance that really was impressive, even to someone who interacted with him daily the way she did.

Timothy Hamilton belonged at the helm of Hamilton Media, she affirmed. The man was a born leader.

Then why am I sad when I think of him sitting

up there in that office, hour after hour, all alone?
she wondered. *He seems happy. Fulfilled. Content
with his role.*

Because I know there's more to life than work,
she answered easily. *There's joy. And peace. And
the love of the Lord that makes everything the best
that it can be.*

That was what she wanted to share with Tim.
Most of the other members of his family seemed to
understand the power of faith, especially since the
onset of Wallace's catastrophic illness. Sometimes
it took a terrible thing like that to strengthen a
person's faith, assuming there was a glimmer of
belief present in the first place.

That was the key, she concluded. And that was
her fear. If Tim didn't believe to start with, there
was nothing she could do to open his mind to the
possibility that God loved him.

Such things were not up to her, nor to anyone
else. If Tim was to be reached, to be comforted, to
be brought into the family of God, the call would
have to come from her Heavenly Father. All she
could do was continue to pray for Tim and try to set
a good example. Beyond that, she was powerless.

Still speaking, Tim introduced a chaplain who
stood to lead a group blessing on the meal.

Dawn bowed her head with the others but sur-
reptitiously watched Tim. He seemed to be partic-
ipating in the prayer. That was a good sign. Now,
if she could just get him to loosen up and attend
church with her, she'd be happy.

That selfish thought settled in her heart like a jagged stone. It wasn't about *her*, it was about *him*. If she truly cared for Tim, and she knew she did, she'd be praying for his personal well-being and happiness, not thinking about what she wanted for herself.

Penitent, Dawn closed her eyes and fought the tears welling behind her lashes. To love, to really love, was to put the other person first. Always. Without reservation.

Such altruism went against human nature but she knew she had to try. For Tim's sake. And her own. Because, in spite of everything, she'd apparently fallen for him.

Chapter Ten

As the dinner got underway, Dawn saw that many of her fears had been groundless. She hadn't tripped or spilled anything and there was little chance she'd accidentally use the wrong fork. The crystal and cutlery were arranged in a logical progression according to need and the only thing confusing was which of the napkins folded into rosettes and tucked into the coffee cups between each place setting was hers. She'd solved that mystery by simply watching which side Tim took his napkin from and following suit.

She was enjoying the salad course immensely until she bit into a rubbery-textured tidbit and looked more closely at the tossed baby greens as she swallowed that mouthful. *Calamari!* Somebody had spiked her salad with squid tentacles! *Ugh.* So much for haute cuisine. She loved seafood in general but definitely drew the line at eating suction cups.

Eyeing Tim, who was not paying the slightest attention to her, she pushed her salad plate away, folded her hands in her lap and waited for the next culinary surprise. Someday, when they were in a more relaxed atmosphere, maybe she'd tell him how proud she was of herself for choking down the disgusting mouthful instead of looking for a graceful way to spit it out!

Tim was eating his own salad while listening to a nearby board member's opinion on stock options. He finally nodded, turned away from the man and smiled at Dawn. "Not hungry?"

"Not very."

"Too much pizza?"

"I guess so."

His mouth quirked in a half smile as he poked through his salad with his fork. "Wish I had some right now. I'm not fond of calamari."

"Neither am I."

Eyeing her rejected plate he immediately asked, "Want me to order you a different salad?"

"No." Dawn shook her head emphatically. "Knowing you, I'd get every scrap of lettuce left in the kitchen—and then some."

Tim chuckled. "I'm not that bad."

"Well…" She was hoping her drawn-out comment would further amuse him and was pleased to see that it did.

"Okay. Maybe I am that bad. But you have to admit I get the job done."

"That, you do."

"Are you having a good time so far?"

Dawn smiled sweetly and leaned closer to speak privately. "Yes, except for making myself swallow that little tentacle I didn't notice hiding in my salad till it was already in my mouth."

She thought Tim was going to choke trying to contain his laughter. He pressed his linen napkin to his lips and coughed into it. "You didn't see it first?"

"Nope."

"It *is* considered a delicacy."

Dawn huffed. "To some people, maybe." She cupped her hand at the side of her mouth to be sure her next comment reached Tim's ears only. "Personally, I'd rather suck the brains out of a boiled crawdad."

That did it. His ears turned red, his eyes widened and moments later he exploded into laughter, muted only by his napkin.

Beside him, Dawn resumed her earlier demure pose, hands in her lap, eyes downcast. She was glad the tablecloth hid her hands from view because she'd had to make fists and press her nails into her palms to keep from laughing along with Tim.

This might have started out like every other stuffy stockholders' dinner he'd ever attended but she imagined this particular evening would stand out in his memory for a very long time. It certainly wasn't a night she'd soon forget.

Penitent, she finally reached to pat him on the back as if she thought he'd choked. There were tears in his eyes and his face was flushed. The coughing lessened. She smiled. "You okay now?"

Tim managed to nod.

"Good." Her smile grew. Her blue eyes sparkled with repressed mischief. "I wasn't kidding, you know. That is how we eat them in Louisiana."

He nodded again and rasped, "I know. That's what made it so funny."

By the time dessert was served, Tim had had many chances to observe Dawn's interaction with their dinner companions. Now that she'd relaxed and was being herself, she was charming everyone around them. She had the same rapport with these people as she'd had with Stuart Meyers, Ada Smith and the others on her meals-on-wheels route.

Perhaps that was the key to her success, Tim reasoned. She didn't discriminate in either direction. Except in his case, he added, chagrined. When it came to money, especially *Hamilton* money, Dawn was definitely biased in the negative. He supposed that was to be expected, since her job as his executive assistant did require a status separation of sorts. Knowing he couldn't be everybody's buddy and still run the company successfully, she had never tried to cross that invisible line. Therefore, it made perfect sense for her to be hesitant to drop their normal office barriers, even in a social situation like this.

It had occurred to him, more than once, that he might have made a serious mistake by inviting her to accompany him and share his standing at the stockholders gala. The decision had been a well-thought-out one but he continued to have misgivings.

It wasn't that he didn't think Dawn belonged wherever she wanted to be. On the contrary, she was holding her own quite admirably. His worry was that getting too familiar with her might harm their exemplary professional relationship.

Tim cleared his throat and watched her with pride. She was a real gem, an asset to his new position, a good right hand to his left. That was the key. They worked together so well they were less like a team than a single entity and he didn't want to lose that edge.

So why had he asked her to accompany him and taken a chance on destroying the working association they'd built? Because he truly enjoyed her company, he admitted. Being with Dawn, listening to her views on life, seeing the way she enjoyed everything so fully, made him feel lighthearted when little else did. He didn't know if she purposely attempted to lift his spirits but that was certainly the result. A person like that—a *woman* like that—was a rare delight. When the family crises were over and the company was on a firmer footing, maybe he'd make an effort to see more of her.

That notion amused Tim. He *saw* Dawn every day in a literal sense. And, in truth, he looked forward to it more all the time. He'd always loved going to work but her presence there made him feel so good he'd found himself sticking his head out of his office and asking her unnecessary questions just to hear her voice and see her smile. She was…

The depth of his musings brought Tim up short. He was beginning to think like a lovesick teenager—like his sister, Melissa, who was the most mixed-up one of them all. Just because Heather had found her dream man in Ethan Danes, Chris was smitten with Felicity Simmons, and Amy had decided to give Bryan Healey another chance, didn't mean all the Hamiltons were ready to settle down. He was only thirty-three. He had plenty of time to find a mate, assuming he wanted one.

Dawn glanced up and caught him staring. "What?"

"Nothing." Tim could feel his cheeks warming. "How's the cheesecake?"

"Delicious." She chuckled softly and whispered, "Not a tentacle in sight. This time, I checked."

"Good for you. I see you're learning."

"How about yours?" Dawn asked with a slight nod toward his dessert. "Don't you like cheese-cake?"

"It's okay." Tim wasn't about to admit he'd been so involved in daydreaming about her he'd forgotten to eat. "I haven't touched it. Would you like it?"

"Umm. I am tempted." She smiled at him and he felt it all the way from the nape of his neck to his toes. "But I think one serving is enough. As short as I am, I don't have a lot of extra room."

"How tall are you?" he asked, mostly to distract himself.

"Five foot three in my bare feet. Much taller in these shoes." She eyed him studiously. "Heather says you're six feet even."

"Yes. Guess I take after Dad."

"I didn't want to ask about him and spoil your mood, but since you've brought it up, how is Wallace doing lately? Do you think he'll be coming home soon?"

"I hope so, especially for my mother's sake. She's beginning to look as weary as he does."

"I know. It's really nice of you to take Nora to lunch the way you do." Dawn paused, frowning. "Why didn't you bring her to this dinner tonight instead of me?"

Not wanting to admit he'd never seriously considered asking his mother, Tim took a slow sip of his after-dinner coffee to buy time to think before answering. "She wouldn't have wanted to come to something like this without Dad, especially since they've always attended as a couple. They've been together for so long they're practically inseparable. Besides, I know she'd have worried about making him feel left out if she'd come."

"My parents are codependent like that in some ways, although my father does go deep-sea fishing without Mom." Dawn sobered. "Lately, she hardly ever goes out because of taking care of my brother, Phil."

"You need to convince her to take some time off.

That's one of the reasons I encourage my mother to go to lunch with me or Heather or the others whenever we're free. Taking breaks is good for her, physically and emotionally."

Dawn was staring at him. Tim frowned. "What?"

A smile started to lift the corners of her mouth and Tim couldn't help noting for the zillionth time how lovely she looked.

"Who are you and what have you done with my boss?"

"I don't understand."

"You can't possibly be Timothy Hamilton," she said with a widening grin. "You just recommended somebody taking time off work. You must be an imposter."

Dawn was so burned-out by the time all the post-dinner speeches, stock market presentations and drawn-out goodbyes were over, she could hardly keep her eyes open during the drive home. Tim seemed to be holding up a lot better than she was, but then he was used to the kind of stressful evening they'd just spent.

"Sleepy?" he asked.

"Um-hum. I feel like I just ran a marathon."

"Do your feet hurt? I notice you took your shoes off."

"Not until I got to the car. I didn't figure you'd be too happy if I left the restaurant carrying them like some hillbilly."

"You can't be a hillbilly," Tim teased. "You're from

the bayous down South." He chuckled. "I thought I'd die laughing when you started talking about how to eat crawdads. I nearly strangled as it was."

Dawn laughed in spite of her weariness. "You should have seen the look on your face! It was priceless."

"You didn't look very good right after you discovered that tentacle, either."

"I was feeling about as green as the lettuce."

"Did you have a good time otherwise?"

"Well, yes, I guess I did," she answered, mildly surprised to realize how true it was. "All that smiling and ultrapolite behavior sure tired me out, though."

"You did a great job."

"Thanks. I'm glad I lived up to expectations so you didn't feel you'd wasted your money on this dress." She gifted him with a tender smile. "You weren't so bad yourself. I guess we made a pretty fair team, huh?"

"I've been thinking about *us,*" Tim said, pausing.

Dawn's heart did a little jig and bounced into her throat. "Us?" The one-word question came out sounding like the squawk of a chicken with its head caught between the slats of a picket fence.

"I mean, we work well together."

"Oh, that. Yes, I guess we do."

"In case I haven't told you lately," Tim said, "I really appreciate all your hard work on behalf of Hamilton Media."

I love you, too, her subconscious offered. "Thanks. I do my best."

"I wouldn't want to lose you."

Just try it, mister. "I'm perfectly happy where I am."

"Good. I need an accomplished assistant like you."

What you need is a poke in the ribs with a sharp stick to wake you up, you dummy. Can't you see I'm crazy about you? She said, "I enjoy the challenge, Mr. Hamilton."

"I thought you were going to call me, Tim?"

You don't want to hear what I'd like to call you right now, she thought, immediately penitent. The poor guy was trying to be nice, to give her compliments on her work ethic which was the most important thing in the world to him, and she wasn't a bit grateful. Well, that couldn't be helped. She'd stupidly fallen for her boss and now she was going to be stuck for who-knows-how-long, trying to keep up the pretense that nothing had changed between them.

"I don't know that it's a good idea for me to call you Tim when we're at the office," Dawn finally said. "It seems awfully personal."

He reached over and laid his warm hand atop hers where it rested on the leather upholstery. "After your performance tonight, I think you've earned it."

Dawn felt as if her hand was afire and her arm was slowly melting, bones and all, like a candle lying too close to a hot oven.

Oh, fine, she thought, giving free rein to her imagination. *There goes my secretarial career. How am I going to type if my arm melts off and I'm left with only five usable fingers?*

She snickered.

Tim pulled away.

"Sorry," she said. "I wasn't laughing at you. I get giddy when I'm overtired. Gabi and I got the giggles one night and were so hysterical we didn't stop laughing till we both had tears running down our cheeks."

"You don't feel one of those fits coming on right now, do you?"

"Don't worry," Dawn said with a shake of her head. "If I do, I'll just dump all those extra hair-brushes out of the bag and stuff my head into it till the urge passes."

Tim's incredulous expression was so funny she did start to chuckle. Clearly, he didn't know how to take her. Well, he wasn't the only befuddled one. She had no idea how to go about getting him to see her as anything but a capable executive assistant—or whether she wanted to try.

He was right about their great working relationship. It was admirable. The question was, what was more important in the grand scheme of things: work or life?

Tim could never answer that because his outlook didn't separate the two, Dawn reminded herself.

Pondering that conclusion she was struck with an even more disturbing thought. Suppose God didn't separate them, either? She'd always believed that the Lord had found her this job in order to put her in a position to help her family financially. If that were the case, how could she argue that life outside the office was all that really mattered?

Confused, Dawn shut her eyes and let the movement of the car coax her closer to sleep. She could have prayed silently but chose not to. If God had any more revelations in store for her she didn't want to be enlightened just yet. One thunderbolt of divine wisdom per night was quite enough, thank you.

After he'd parked in front of Dawn's apartment in Hickory Mills, Tim watched her sleeping for long seconds, then woke her with gentle words and a light touch on her shoulder. "Dawn? You're home."

She stirred. Her lashes fluttered against her cheeks like tiny butterflies. She opened her eyes, looked at him and began to smile. "Hi."

Even in the dim reflection of the streetlight her smile was enough to warm him all the way to his soul. "Good morning. Did you sleep well?"

"Um-hum." She stretched and yawned. "Sorry I conked out on you."

"That's okay. I figured it was safer to let you sleep than wake you and chance the female hysterics you'd warned me about."

"Smart man." Gathering up her purse and slipping a finger through the straps at the heels of her shoes she reached for the door handle.

Tim's hand brushed her forearm, careful to keep his touch gentle and undemanding. "Wait. I'll get the door and walk you up."

"Are we back to that again? I can manage. Honest."

"Humor me? I'm not doing it because I think it's my duty, I'm doing it because I want to."

Her eyes widened. "Okay."

The fall night air was chilly when he got out. Tim slipped off his jacket as he rounded the car and held it ready to place around her shoulders.

He'd thought, from her body language as she stood, that she was going to resist the chivalrous gesture but she didn't. He laid the jacket across her shoulders and held it there as they walked into the building. Then, she stepped ahead of him to climb the stairs.

He'd seen·that her building was quiet and safe the last time he'd brought her there, so what had made him insist he walk her all the way to her door again? Manners dictated, of course, yet it was more than that. A lot more. It surprised him to realize he didn't want their time together to end. Somehow, sometime during the evening, the focus had shifted from business to pleasure. He'd actually enjoyed every minute of his time with Dawn, so much so that he wanted to prolong it.

She paused at her door and quickly found her key ring in the small clutch. Tim took the keys from her and unlocked her door but made no move to push it open for fear of repeating his initial encounter with her dog.

"Well, I guess this is good-night," she said quietly.

"Yes." He took her hand, turned it over and placed the keys in her palm. Instead of letting go, he continued to cradle her small hand as he said, "I had an amazing evening. Thank you for keeping me company."

"It was my pleasure," Dawn said. "And thank you for the dress."

"You should thank Heather."

Dawn was gazing into his eyes and smiling sweetly. "What Heather did, she did on your orders. And with your money. Lots of it. I'm just glad I was able to keep the costs down as much as I did."

"It was worth every penny. That dress—you—are beautiful."

She reclaimed her hand, used it to swing his jacket off her shoulders and handed the coat to him. "Thank you. You're not so hard to look at, yourself…Tim."

Stepping back, he hooked a finger in the collar of the tuxedo jacket and slung it casually over one shoulder. "See you Monday, then."

"Yes, unless…" He watched her apparently struggle to decide whether or not to go on before she said, "We're having a potluck after the evening church service at Northside tomorrow. Drop in if you'd like to taste some great, old-fashioned, home-cooked food. We'd love to have you."

"No crawdads?"

Dawn shook her head and smiled more broadly. "Nope. Usually just ham and maybe fried chicken. If you want Cajun delicacies you'll have to go a lot farther South."

"Or wait till you make another pot of that soup. It really was good."

"I'm glad you liked it. Well…"

"Right." He took another tentative step backward. "Good night, Dawn."

He watched her turn, enter her apartment and close the door behind her before he started back down the stairs. He hadn't quite reached the second floor landing when he heard a shriek, followed by his name.

"Tim!"

Dawn! Every instinct to protect her came to full alert. His nostrils flared. His heart pounded. Whirling, he raced back up the steps two at a time.

When he hit the third floor, there she was, waiting for him in the dimly lit hallway! And she appeared to be alone. *Thank God!*

Tim grabbed her upper arms, held her fast. "What is it? What's wrong?"

Wide-eyed, she held out the velvet jewelry box. "Your mother's necklace. I forgot to give it back to you."

Tim felt as if a belligerent giant had punched him in the stomach and knocked all the air out of his lungs.

Still grasping her arms he leaned his head back, closed his eyes and took a deep, settling breath. "Is that all? I thought…"

"I'm so sorry," Dawn said. "I panicked when I got inside and saw the empty box sitting there. Please, take the diamonds with you?"

"Sure."

Reluctant to let her go he turned her, then forced

himself to relax his hold. "Lift your hair so I can see the clasp."

As she did so, her silky tresses brushed his cheek and sent a shiver down his spine.

He made short work of the necklace and swung it free so he could distance himself before he gave in to the growing urge to really embrace her. He didn't know when he'd been that frightened and all he wanted to do was celebrate his relief by holding her tight and kissing her senseless.

Instead, he got control of his emotions and stepped away. "There. Can you handle the earrings?"

"Yes."

Dawn passed him the velvet box to hold while she fumbled with the screw-back posts. When she'd removed both earrings she secured the backs and laid them carefully in the box with the necklace.

Watching her, Tim was getting the impression she hated the jewelry, was loathe to even touch it. He snapped the box closed and slid it into his pocket. There was enough extra adrenaline coursing through his veins to keep him up half the night. That, coupled with his frustration, wasn't helping his mood.

"If you're done screaming and scaring me to death, go lock yourself in your apartment with your watchdog, where it's safe," Tim said, physically turning her once more so she faced her door. "I'm going home."

He gave her a nudge, watched her go inside, then waited till he heard the latch click into place. He didn't know when he'd been more frightened. Probably never. The idea that something terrible might have happened to Dawn churned in his gut and rose like bile in his throat.

"Women," he grumbled. If they weren't driving you crazy they were scaring you to death.

Chapter Eleven

Dawn would have phoned Gabi for a session of serious girl-talk right after Tim left if it hadn't been so late. Although she overslept the following morning and had to drag herself to church she still managed to arrive on time to teach Sunday school, as usual.

Gabi met her in the hallway outside their respective classrooms and greeted her enthusiastically. "Well? How did it go?"

"Fine. I had a great time."

"That's it? That's all? No way, Jose. Come on. Spill it. I want all the details."

"Well, let's see." Dawn struck a pose, index finger lying beside her cheek. "I didn't fall off my shoes. I didn't barf when I accidentally swallowed a squid tentacle. I didn't lose the borrowed diamond jewelry, but I did scare Tim silly when I hollered at him to come back and get it. I ate real cheesecake and loved every bite." She paused. "Oh, and I decided I was in love with my boss."

"What?" Gabi's jaw dropped and she stared, openmouthed.

"Yup." Dawn gave a little shrug. "You heard me. I think I love Tim Hamilton. Ain't that the pits?"

"You just got swept off your feet by the romantic mood last night," Gabi argued. "Did he make a move on you? Try to kiss you?"

"No. He was a perfect gentleman. That's part of the problem. He was so polite it made me wonder if I had spinach stuck to my teeth or something."

"Did you?"

"We didn't even eat spinach. I was making a joke."

Gabi frowned and shook her head. "The joke is how you could think you were in love *already*. You've only had one real date with the guy."

"Yes, but I've seen him every weekday for nearly a year. I just never viewed him as anything but my boss until he murdered my car and drove me around with the meals-on-wheels deliveries."

"One good deed does not make Tim Hamilton a hero."

"It's a lot more than that," Dawn said. "If you take the time to look beneath his polished exterior there's a heart of gold. Remember how he befriended Stuart?"

"Lots of people at Northside take care of others. It's what this church does. That's not special, it's normal."

"For us it is. For somebody like Tim, it isn't. He's

usually all business. Altruism is a big change for him. You said so yourself. There was no profit in it and he was still nice to a lonely old man."

"Fine. Give him a medal. Just don't throw your heart away because of one or two glimmers of decency."

"I haven't thrown anything away," Dawn said seriously. "Tim doesn't have a clue how I feel. Nobody knows but you and me, and that's the way I plan to keep it. The last thing I need is for him to suspect I care about him—at least until he shows me he may share those feelings."

"Sounds like the kind of crush a teenager gets," Gabi said. "If we were still in high school, you could always wait till Tim offers to carry your books between classes and then you'd know he was interested in you."

"Very funny."

"Actually, no, it isn't." Her friend sighed. "Maybe you ought to have a talk with Pastor Abernathy."

"Charles David Abernathy has plenty to do without my bothering him about my feelings for my boss."

"Oh? And what do you suppose he feels is more important than the welfare of his flock?"

"I don't know." The six- and-seven-year-olds in her class had started to arrive so Dawn lowered her voice to continue their adult discussion. "I feel the same way about bothering God with trivial stuff. Know what I mean?"

"Sure," Gabi said wisely. "Would you care to tell

me what you think is important to Him? He made
the universe, Dawn. He created the cosmos.
Nothing is too big or too small for God."

"You do have a point. I'll think about it, okay?"

Gabi paused to give her a quick hug. "Okay. And
I'll go ahead and pray you come to your senses, if
you don't mind."

Dawn smiled. "Pray away, sister. I need all the
divine guidance I can get."

"Now *that* we agree on."

Tim had an early tee time Sunday morning. His
game was off but he blamed it on the stresses of the
previous evening. Images of Dawn kept popping
into his head and refused to go away, even when he
was trying to sink a difficult putt. He finished the
back nine but his score was dismal. He hadn't ended
up that many strokes over par in years and took an
awful teasing from his partners, Richard McNeil
among them.

"Hey, nobody's perfect," Tim countered as they
headed for their cars in the clubhouse parking lot.
"Not even me, although I do have my moments of
greatness."

"Yeah," McNeil said. "Like last night. You were
sure in your element presiding over that bunch of
investors."

"Thanks."

"Of course, you also had the best-looking
woman in Tennessee keeping you company, so
you should have been riding high. Smooth,

buddy. Real smooth. Too bad you don't play golf that well."

"Yeah." His companions laughed and Tim joined them rather than express his disappointment in his apparent loss of skill. Another morning like this one and he'd be ready to sell his clubs and take up a game he could win.

Winning was what mattered most, he told himself. Unlike hobbyists such as Stuart Meyers, he didn't keep refighting the same battles. If he lost, as he had this morning, then he accepted it, put it behind him and moved on. There was nothing to be gained by rehashing failures until they drove you crazy.

Thoughts of failing made him clench his teeth and focus on his family. He waved goodbye to Richard, tossed his golf bag into the trunk of his car and slammed the lid closed. Maybe he'd swing by the hospital and say hello to his father before he went home, instead of coming back later during visiting hours.

The vision of Wallace's deteriorating condition made his stomach clench. Every time Tim saw the once-virile man in that hospital bed it was harder to take. After the experiences of the past few months, just walking in the door of Community General and smelling the antiseptic air made him ill.

Tim took a deep breath and steeled himself. There were many things he didn't relish doing, yet duty forced him to face them head-on. This wasn't a game like golf, it was a real life-or-death battle. Tim knew no one lived forever but he couldn't get his mind around the concept of his father's eventual death. It was simply unacceptable.

Driving away from the golf course, Tim dialed his mother's cell phone number. She answered on the first ring.

"Are you at the hospital?"

"Yes. I've been here since right after church. Heather and Amy were, too, but they left."

"I'll be there in about fifteen minutes. How's Dad doing?"

He could tell by the muted sound that Nora had cupped her hand around the receiver's mouthpiece. "Better, I think. Dr. Strickland gave him something to help him sleep. He's so weak, but he won't quit fighting to stay awake."

"Do you think it would be better if I visited later?"

"Probably."

Tim's conscience knotted, arguing that it was wrong to be glad of the reprieve. "Okay," he said. "How about you? Are you going home soon? Can I take you out for Sunday dinner?"

"Not today, honey," Nora said. "I'm just going to rest here until your father wakes up."

Tim had assumed those would be her plans but had felt compelled to ask. "Call me when he's up to having company, will you? I want to tell him how well the get-together at Opryland went last night."

"Good news only, I hope. It would be hard on him to hear otherwise."

"Very good. Everything's fine. He'll be pleased."

"What about your date? Did that go well, too?"

"It wasn't a date," Tim argued. "I simply took my executive assistant with me to help her get acquainted with some of the board members and important stockholders."

"Of course you did, dear. Heather tells me the dress she and Dawn picked out was sort of silvery."

"Heather must be color-blind. It was blue, the same as Dawn's eyes." He thought he heard his mother snicker. "What's so funny?"

"You are," Nora said. "You're so busy trying to fill your father's shoes, you're overlooking the part of him I love the most—his zest for living. If he were really the consummate business tycoon you seem to think he was, he'd have had a booming media company and that's all."

"Meaning?" Tim swung his car onto Highway 24, headed north.

"Meaning, where do you think you children came from, baskets on our doorstep?"

Tim refrained from mentioning Jeremy's origins even though that was the first thought that popped into his head. Instead, he turned the erstwhile maternal lecture into a joking exchange by saying, "I don't know about myself, Mom, but I've often wondered if you got Melissa from some passing vagabonds. She sure has the wanderlust."

"Melissa will be fine. She was raised right and she'll remember that eventually," Nora said. "I'm proud of all my children. You're individuals but you're still a family. I'd admire you kids even if we weren't related."

Even the black sheep among us? Tim wondered. *Undoubtedly.* Nora was a better person than he was. That notion made him smile. Of course she was. Mothers were supposed to be models of proper behavior, even if they slipped now and then.

He said, "Thanks, Mom. I'm passing the off-ramp to the hospital. You sure you don't want to go grab a bite with me while Dad's sleeping?"

"No, thanks. I'm fine. I may stop off at Northside on my way home tonight. They're having a potluck."

"So Dawn said."

"Oh? Are you going?"

"I hadn't planned on it."

"Why don't you come? You can pick me up so I won't have to drive."

"You're a better driver than I am," Tim countered.

"True. I haven't damaged any cars lately. I just thought, if I could count on you to take me over there, I wouldn't have to worry about dozing off at the wheel. I really am beat."

"I know you are." Tim was penitent. "All right. What time do you want me to come and get you?"

"A little before six will be fine. At the house. And Tim? Stop off at the grocery store and pick up some bags of chips or something like that, will you? Vera Mae has the day off so I can't ask her to fix anything and we don't want to show up empty-handed."

"Okay." He sighed noisily. "I need to give back

your necklace, anyway. I'll see you around five-thirty, quarter to six."

"Fine. After church we can come visit your father together."

"Church?" His brow knit. "I thought you said we were going there for a meal."

"We are. There'll just be a short service first. It won't kill you."

"It might," he grumbled. "If the roof caves in because I'm there, I won't be responsible."

His mother laughed warmly. "I'll take my chances."

Dawn had volunteered to help in the kitchen so she wasn't in the sanctuary to see Tim arrive. The first she heard of it was when Gabi rushed up to her and announced the surprising news.

"He's here!" Gabi shouted, crossing the fellowship hall at a trot and pointing. "Right out there, big as life."

Dawn frowned. "Who is?"

"Tim Hamilton, that's who."

"You're kidding!"

Gabi pressed her hand to her throat and struck a pose of innocence. "I do not kid about things like that. He just walked in."

"I'd better go welcome him, then." She started to untie her apron.

"He's not alone. He's with his mother," Gabi said, handing two bulging plastic grocery sacks to one of the other workers. "They gave me these."

"Oh." Dawn felt deflated. "I thought maybe he came because I invited him."

"Maybe he did. Who knows? At least he's here."

"That's true." She eyed the sacks. "One thing is for sure. Tim bought that stuff. He's big on over-supply. Which reminds me. I have new hairbrushes for the girls and you. Lots of them. I left them in Tim's car but I'm sure he'll return them to me."

"Hairbrushes?"

Dawn was sorry she'd mentioned the brushes because that meant she'd have to confess what had happened to her fancy hairdo. "It's a long story. I felt funny with my hair up so I decided to take it down— sorry—only I didn't have a brush with me. Tim went into a store to buy me one and came out with dozens of them." She smiled. "It was kind of sweet, actually. He said he wanted me to have a choice."

"Sounds like a guy who can't make up his mind to me."

"Cynic."

"Oh, I don't know. Look at all the chips he bought."

"They'll be put to good use. What we don't eat tonight we can serve to the youth group as snacks when they meet. See? God provided."

"No, Tim Hamilton provided. I refuse to believe that God has any influence over that man."

Sobering, Dawn sighed before she said, "I sure hope you're wrong about that. I truly do."

Dawn fidgeted for the entire twenty-five minutes it took for Pastor Abernathy to address the congregation, ask the blessing on the food and dismiss everyone to eat. Although she'd assured herself she'd play it cool when she saw Tim, she broke into a silly, elated grin the moment she spotted him.

"Down, girl," Gabi warned.

"Oh, hush. I'm not going to do anything stupid."

"Don't count on it. I doubt most folks would look that pleased if the President of the United States walked in and grabbed a plate."

Dawn had to agree. This was the first time she'd seen Tim dressed casually. Even during his visit to Stuart's, when he'd removed his jacket and tie to make it easier to stage the war, he'd still started out looking like a high-powered executive.

Tonight, however, in keeping with the more relaxed atmosphere of the evening service, he was wearing khaki slacks and a polo shirt. Dawn assumed that Nora must have told him about the unwritten dress code for the evening service because she couldn't imagine Tim going anywhere without a necktie.

Wearing a tie had always looked uncomfortable and seemed silly to her, especially in hot weather. In that respect, women were far more liberated than men, weren't they? If they didn't want to wear a stiff collar and knot a piece of fabric around their necks like a noose, they simply didn't do it.

The parishioners formed a line and slowly filed past the buffet-style arrangement of food. Dawn, Gabi and three others waited aside, ready to remove an empty dish and replace it with another that hadn't fit on the crammed serving tables initially.

She was trying so hard to avoid looking at Tim she almost missed seeing his mother's smile of recognition.

Nora approached, carrying her plate. "Hello there! I wondered why I didn't see you out front. Did you have a good time last night?"

"Wonderful. Thank you so much for letting me borrow your beautiful jewelry."

"You're more than welcome to wear it any time you want," Nora said amiably. "With the exception of last night, it hasn't been out of the safe for over a year. Seems a shame not to wear it but I don't go out much anymore."

"You will again. We're all praying for Wallace's recovery."

Tears misted in Nora's eyes. "Thank you. That means a lot to us."

"All of you?" Dawn glanced at Tim. Still in line, he'd just chosen a slice of ham and was busy piling chips onto his paper plate beside it.

Nora nodded. "Some men are quieter about their faith than others. Wallace was more like Tim until recently. Just because Tim doesn't get on a soapbox about what he believes doesn't mean there's nothing deep there. Give him time. You'll see."

"It's really none of my business," Dawn said.

"I wouldn't be so sure. I must have invited my son to come to church with me and the family a hundred times. He didn't accept until after he'd spent time with you. Seems to me you have to take some of the credit."

"I just want to see him happy," Dawn said quietly. "Ever since I came to work for him, he's struck me as kind of a loner."

"He tends to be a private person," Nora explained. "Jeremy, Chris and the girls have always been more gregarious than Tim. He's my serious one. A man like that can always be trusted to tell you the truth, regardless of the consequences." She smiled. "In some cases, that's a definite advantage, don't you think?"

"I…" Before Dawn could answer fully, Tim joined them. One look at him and her mind was wiped so clean of coherent thought she was surprised she could manage an intelligible greeting. "Hi."

"Hello." Tim gifted her with a broad smile. "I see you have another talent you didn't tell me about."

"Huh?"

"Kitchen staff? You are working here, aren't you? I saw the apron and I assumed…"

"I help out once in a while."

"Do they let you sit down and eat? We can save you a place at our table."

She shook her head. "We all grabbed a bite beforehand."

"Okay." He turned his attention to his mother and began shepherding her toward an empty table. Dawn heard him ask Nora, "What can I get you to drink?" before she ducked into the kitchen and flattened her back against a wall.

Gabi trailed her. "What's wrong? You sick?"

"Yeah. Sick of myself," Dawn muttered. "Did you hear me babbling out there? I hardly knew my own name."

"I heard you talking to Mrs. Hamilton. You seemed okay then."

"I was, until Tim walked up. Then I sounded like a dunce. He asked me to sit with them and I told him we'd eaten."

"Well, we have. We always snack while we wait. What's wrong with that?"

Dawn rolled her eyes. "Nothing. Nothing at all. Except that I could have taken off my apron and at least sat with them. Instead, I acted like the poor man had invited me to a hanging or something."

"I doubt it was that bad." Gabi was chuckling and staring at her as if she were deluded. "Look, if it's that important to you, why don't you go keep them company? It's not too late."

"Sure it is. I already begged off. I could kick myself."

"Please, not on church property," Gabi teased. "It'd be bad for Northside's image if folks started going home from our services all bruised."

Dawn shot her a derisive look. "Yeah, right. I'm in the middle of a crisis here and you're cracking dumb jokes."

"Oh, go get a piece of pie or something and take it to their table. Trust me. They won't think it's strange."

"They won't?"

"Of course not. That is, if you really want to

spend a few minutes with them. Sure looks to me like you do."

"I don't want to seem pushy."

"Nonsense." Gabi peeked around the corner. "Heather's there with Ethan and Amy brought Bryan and Dylan. Tim and Nora make seven, so there's still an empty place at their table. If you hurry...uh-oh."

Dawn stiffened. "What?"

"See for yourself. Lauralee Seeger just grabbed the last chair."

"Lauralee? Where? Let me look." Leaning around Gabi, Dawn made a sound of disgust. "Humph. If she scooted any closer to Tim she'd be sitting in his lap."

"I know. And he looks pretty uncomfortable about it. Too bad. If you hadn't stood here arguing with me, you'd be in that chair."

Dawn whipped off her apron and shoved it at Gabi. "Here. Cover for me."

"Where are you going?"

"To the rescue," Dawn said. "This is the first time Tim's been in church for ages and I'm not going to let somebody like Lauralee scare him off."

"Atta girl." Gabi giggled. "Every congregation needs a few superheroes to step up and make things right."

Behind her, Dawn could hear Gabi working into a good belly laugh. She snagged a piece of pie and a plastic fork as she passed the assorted desserts and never missed a step.

Arriving at Tim's table with a wide, innocent

grin firmly in place she tapped Lauralee on the shoulder. "Excuse me? I believe you're in my seat."

The other woman twisted to scowl up at her. "Nobody was sitting here."

"I just went to get some pie," Dawn said. "I'm sorry my friends didn't mention it before you got settled." She put her dessert on the table so her hands would be free. "Here. I'll help you get moved. No, no, don't thank me. Glad to do it." She grabbed the woman's plate and cup of lemonade and started to walk away with them. "Here we go. I think I see an empty place by Pastor Abernathy. Yes, I do. You're in luck."

Tim was chuckling behind his napkin when Dawn returned a few seconds later. "Nice save," he said as he held the chair for her.

"Thanks. You looked like you might appreciate a little breathing room."

Across the table, Nora was actually snickering. "I thought Tim was going to need some of his father's bottled oxygen before that girl was through. Talk about desperate!"

"Hey, I was the desperate one," Tim said. "Thankfully, not all the women in my life are like that."

"Hear, hear," Heather cheered, winking at Ethan, the newspaper photographer who had stolen her heart. "We wouldn't want to see you settle down or anything."

Ethan played along. "No way, man. Besides, who would take your wedding pictures if Heather and I are away on our honeymoon?"

That comment made Tim's cheeks rosy. He cleared his throat. "Can the wedding talk, Ethan. I'm a long way from being ready for anything like that." He cast a sidelong glance at the table where Dawn had deposited the hopeful other woman. "Especially lately."

"Then again," Nora piped up, "you never know. The perfect woman might be right under your nose and you just won't admit it."

Chapter Twelve

Tim had given his mother's comment about recognizing the right woman more consideration than he liked during the following week. He couldn't seem to get the notion out of his head. The only suitable candidate he could imagine in any scenario was Dawn Leroux.

Admittedly, he and Dawn came from diverse backgrounds, yet she was intelligent and openminded. Perhaps, if he gave her a more in-depth view of his life away from the office, they could tell if their relationship had potential. It was worth a try. All he had to do was come up with something they could do together that was indicative of his interests without being business-oriented.

Days later, he was still mulling over the problem. The amazing thing was how little he actually did that wasn't somehow tied to Hamilton Media. Finally, he settled on golf. It was a nonthreatening pastime and would get them out of their usual haunts without giving Dawn the impression he was actually courting her. If and when the time came for getting serious, he'd ask her out on real dates. For now, a turn on the golf course would be fun, and since she'd never played before, he'd have the opportunity to teach her about the game, too.

The ideal occasion was coming up in a little over two weeks, Tim realized. There was a local tournament on the schedule at the country club where he always played. That would do. He'd casually mention the event to Dawn and see what her reaction was before making solid plans.

Tim was about to call her into his office and open conversation regarding the golf outing when his sister Amy popped in and distracted him.

"Morning," Amy said. "There was a message on my voice mail that you wanted to see me."

"I do."

She approached his desk. "Okay, what's up?"

"I've been thinking."

"Uh-oh. Sounds serious."

"It is. I've think we've been patient long enough. It's time we contacted a private detective about bringing Melissa home."

"That isn't necessary."

"Yes, it is. Dad's getting pretty worried. He doesn't say much about it but I know him."

"I'll have a talk with him and calm his fears," Amy said. "Trust me. Melissa's fine."

"How can you be so sure?" Watching his sister's

expression, Tim concluded that she knew more than she was admitting.

"I told you I'd talked to her," Amy said defensively.

"Not recently, you didn't. Has she called again?"

"Yes."

"Well, why didn't you *say* so?" Tim knew his voice was raised but he was too upset to care.

"Melissa asked me not to tell anybody. I respected her wishes."

"What about the rest of us? What about *our* feelings?

Amy shook her head sadly. "She made me promise to keep her call a secret. What could I do?"

"I don't believe this. Why *you?* Why didn't she call the house?"

"Probably because she didn't want to take the chance of getting a lecture if Mom or Dad answered instead of Heather. If I were her, I know that's the last thing I'd have wanted."

"Is she okay?"

"Relatively. I suspect she'll be heading home soon. Sounds to me like she and Dean aren't getting along very well anymore."

"It's about time she saw him for the creep he is."

"That's what I told her."

"Terrific."

Tim was about to deliver a tirade worthy of their father when Dawn rapped on the half-open door, stuck her head in and said, "Excuse me?"

"What is it?" In spite of Tim's efforts to temper his reply it came out sounding terse.

"Your ten o'clock appointment is waiting," Dawn said, indicating with an exaggerated roll of her eyes that the other party was close by. "If you two are going to continue to discuss your sister, you might want to close this door."

"I was just going," Amy said. "I have a magazine to run and deadlines to meet." She breezed past Dawn, giving her a wink as she passed. "See ya."

Tim was miffed but he saw no advantage to insisting he and Amy finish their conversation at that time. Later, when he had a free moment, he'd visit her in her own office and find out what else she might be keeping from him. In the meantime, he had a company to run.

Straightening the knot of his tie and smoothing the lapels of his jacket, Tim calmed himself. "All right. You can send in the ten o'clock, Ms. Leroux. And as soon as we're finished, I'd like a private word with you."

"Yes, sir." She lowered her voice to speak aside to him. "I couldn't help overhearing. I'm sorry."

"That's not why I want to see you," Tim said. "And before you ask me again, no, I am *not* planning to fire you over it. Okay?"

He was rewarded with one of her typical grins. "Yes, sir. That's good to know. Thanks."

"Don't mention it."

As she left his office, Tim found himself mirroring her infectious smile and feeling a whole lot more lighthearted in spite of everything that had just occurred.

That was what seeing Dawn always did to him. Especially lately. It didn't mean anything, of course. Lots of people had the innate ability to make others feel good. That preacher, Abernathy, was one of them, too. His welcoming words and handshake when they'd met at the potluck at Northside had been so genuine it had taken Tim by surprise. The guy was a great salesman, even if Tim wasn't buying the Pollyanna attitude he was peddling.

The door opened. His appointment entered. Tim offered his hand and a pleasant greeting.

Pushing other thoughts aside and getting down to business had always been one of Tim's natural gifts. This time, however, he found himself struggling to concentrate on the subject at hand. That was disquieting. So was his subconscious dread that something in his life—something important—wasn't quite right.

If Dawn hadn't had so much to do at her desk she'd have given in to the urge to pace while she waited to find out why Tim wanted to see her privately. Lots of possibilities came to mind. Thankfully, since he'd vowed he didn't intend to fire her, the choices weren't all that dire.

She smiled and shook her head in self-derision. She didn't know why that negative idea kept popping into her head. Maybe it was because she'd grown up listening to her parents fret over a lack of steady work for her father. Those had been hard times.

Oh, they'd tried to hide their concern from her and

Phil, but she and her brother had both figured it out pretty quickly. Kids weren't stupid. And now that Phil was dependent upon their parents for nearly everything, her continuing employment was a critical factor in the whole family's well-being. Little wonder she tended to worry about job security.

Dawn closed her eyes for an instant, fingers resting on the edge of the computer keyboard. "Thank You, God, for finding me a job I love and one that makes such good use of my skills."

Tim's office door clicked open. She alerted and smiled at the departing client. "I trust everything went well?"

"Fine, fine." He dismissed her with a wave of his hand as if she were a pesky mosquito and stalked out.

"And good morning to you, too," she muttered as soon as he was out of hearing range. "I'm certainly glad I'm not your executive assistant."

The intercom buzzed. "Dawn? Please come in now."

"Yes, sir." She gathered pad and pencil and paused a moment to dig up her wayward smile before she squared her shoulders and entered Tim's private office.

"Sit down," he said, indicating a leather side chair.

"Okay." Tim looked grim. Whatever was bothering him seemed to be serious, at least in his opinion. Chances were good he was still stewing over Amy's visit. It would be just like him to dwell on something negative like that.

"Have you placed all the employees from accounting?"

The question caught her off guard. She frowned slightly. "Yes, sir. I put that information on your desk last week."

"Right, right. I do remember seeing it. Good job."

Watching him twist a pen in his right hand and sensing the tension he was trying to hide, Dawn wondered what had him so dithered. Had she committed some error he was stewing about? Had she unknowingly offended a client? Had she…?

Oh, stop, she told herself. *Imagining things like that is stupid. If Tim had a problem with your work he'd simply say so. He has before.*

She folded her hands in her lap and forced herself to display outward patience. Tim Hamilton wasn't one for wasting time. Surely, he'd get to the point soon.

"There's a golf tournament coming up at the country club," he finally said.

Dawn smiled. "That's nice. Are you playing in it?"

"I hadn't intended to participate but I do plan to watch. I wondered if you might like to go with me."

"Golf?" She tried not to look incredulous.

"Sure. Why not? You're always saying you're open to learning new things."

"I am. I'm just a little surprised, that's all."

"Then it's settled. It's a week from Sunday." He leaned forward to make a note on his desk calendar. "The first team tees off at eight so I'll pick you up at seven-thirty, sharp. Wear walking shoes. And bring a hat. Even in October the sun can be brutal."

She scowled. "It's when?"

Tim glanced at the calendar pages he'd just leafed through and cited the exact date.

Sunday. It echoed in her whirling thoughts. More importantly, Sunday morning. Didn't he realize that was the only time she wasn't available, or didn't he care? That was the most likely assumption. Tim saw no good reason to go to church so he'd summarily discounted her commitment. She knew how his mind worked—if worship wasn't important to him, why should it be important to anyone else?

She shouldn't have been taken aback or disappointed by his selfishness but she was, just the same. Getting to her feet and facing him across the desk she forced herself to act calm and polite. "Sorry. But thanks for asking."

"What?"

She remained firm, shoulders back, chin jutted. Obviously, the man was not used to being turned down. Well, too bad. It was about time somebody stood up to him and his high-and-mighty opinions of himself. There was more to life than pleasing Tim Hamilton, and if she'd been appointed to demonstrate that salient fact, then so be it.

"I said *no*." Turning, she started for the door then paused to glance pointedly at her watch. "It's nearly lunchtime. I'll be out of the office for the next forty-five minutes or so."

Swinging by her desk, she hesitated only long

enough to pull her purse from the bottom drawer and grab her keys. All she wanted to do was get out of there before she wept. Anger did that to her. Come to think of it, most strong emotions made her cry. It was a trait she considered a fault but one over which she had little control.

Disillusionment filled her heart and soul, robbing her of rational thought. Tim had seemed to be coming along so well, to be accepting the faith she and his family shared. But she'd been fooling herself, hadn't she, by wishing for a change in his attitude toward worship. How much had she simply imagined because it was what she wanted to see?

Probably plenty, she decided. Whoever had said *love is blind* had certainly had the right idea.

Tim sat at his desk and watched Dawn flounce out of the room. He was dumbfounded. What in the world had set her off like that?

Getting slowly to his feet he walked to the window that looked down on the employee parking lot. It didn't take long to spot Dawn. She came out of the door and ran to her car as if she were being chased by a swarm of killer bees. What was wrong with her?

Tim cursed under his breath. *Her?* What was wrong with *him* to think she might care, might actually want to spend quality time with him? Clearly, that was not the case.

He turned away, trying not to worry about her safety as she sped out of the lot. So she wasn't interested in developing a relationship. So what? He knew from experience that there were plenty of others who were. If he ever decided to marry he wouldn't have to try very hard to find a suitable partner.

Only simple suitability wasn't enough anymore, Tim realized with a start. He wanted a soul mate, not just any willing partner. Considering his own financial position and his family's collective wealth he knew he'd have trouble weeding out the fortune hunters, too. What he wanted, what he needed, was a woman who liked him for himself and didn't care about the money. A woman who saw his prosperity as a detriment, not an asset. A woman who had character and high moral principles. A woman like Dawn Leroux.

Disgusted, he sat back down and stared at the walls, unseeing. Every word of their last conversation was as clear as if he'd recorded it for playback. For the life of him, he couldn't spot one error in anything he'd said or done.

Tim snorted in disgust. What good was an analytical mind if the actions of all parties weren't equally logical? What good was *anything?*

Dawn drove straight to the hospital administrative offices to see Gabi. She didn't even slow down at the reception desk, plunging instead into her best friend's presence unannounced.

"Whoa! You look awful," Gabi said, rising to meet her with a hug. "Who died?"

That little bit of compassion was all it took to set

Dawn off. Tears rolled down her cheeks. "I feel like I did," she blubbered. "I thought…I thought…"

"Sit down, blow your nose, pull yourself together and tell me about it," Gabi said tenderly. "Whatever it is, it can't be that bad."

"Oh, yes it can." Those words triggered more shuddering sobs as Dawn fought to regain control of her turbulent emotions. Finally she managed to add, "Tim asked me out."

"Oh, well, that explains it. The cad. How dare he want to see you socially."

Dawn grimaced. "It's not funny."

"It is from where I'm sitting," Gabi said. "What's so bad about having another date with him? I thought you had a blast at that fancy dinner he took you to."

"I did. But mostly because Tim was there." She sniffled and blotted her tears.

"So? What's wrong?"

"He wanted me to go to a golf tournament on Sunday morning."

"Okay. I can see the problem with that. What did he say when you told him you were busy then?"

"I didn't."

"What? Why not?"

"Because he should know me better than that. I've never made any secret of my involvement at Northside. Of my commitment. When he asked me to go somewhere on a Sunday, it was clear he didn't care."

Gabi rolled her eyes. "Oh, brother."

"Well, it was. Look at it from my point of view. Every time our church meets I see dozens of women who are there by themselves because their husbands refuse to come. I don't want to join their ranks. Period. It doesn't matter why they're alone, they just are. And it's so sad."

"Some are widows, like me," Gabi said softly.

"Oh, honey." Dawn gave her a brief hug and grabbed another handful of tissues. "I know that. I don't mean those who have no choice. I'm talking about the women who knew their partner wasn't interested in sharing their faith and married him, anyway."

"I'm sure some had no idea."

"That's true. And I'm not saying they don't have great marriages in every other way. A lot of them do. I'm just not going to put myself in that same position when I can already tell that Tim doesn't value my beliefs."

"Okay. I guess you're right."

"You know I am. Remember the verse about being unequally yoked?"

"Among others. Look. It's almost time for my lunch break. What do you say we both go drown our sorrows in enough chocolate to give us zits?"

Dawn's reddened eyes widened as she realized exactly what her friend had implied. "Oh, dear. I've been thinking only of myself. I'm sorry. What's wrong?"

"Nothing new," Gabi said with a short laugh. "I'm just taking advantage of this opportunity to pig out without guilt. Friends should never let friends eat medicinal chocolate alone. It's practically a law."

"If it isn't, it ought to be," Dawn agreed. She blew her nose and disposed of the tissue in Gabi's wastebasket. "Thanks for being so understanding."

"Hey, I'm a sucker for a love story."

Dawn huffed. "My relationship with Tim is hardly that."

"Maybe not yet," Gabi said. "But I'm starting to see that nothing is impossible for God."

"Who brought *Him* into this?"

Gabi laughed. "You did, kiddo. The minute you put going to church above your own desires you chose up sides. There's nothing wrong with being dedicated. Nothing at all."

"But?"

"But, you might want to keep in mind that the Lord really does work in mysterious ways. If I were you, I'd want to make mighty sure I was in God's will before I cut myself off from Tim Hamilton simply because he made one little mistake."

"It wasn't little. It was a biggie."

Watching her friend's dark eyes sparkle with repressed mirth, Dawn heard her say, "Big to you, maybe. I doubt it was even a hiccup in God's opinion."

Chapter Thirteen

Dawn dreaded having to go back to work after lunch. If she hadn't felt that it would be dishonest, she'd have called in sick. Truth to tell, she and Gabi had binged on so much junk food she didn't feel all that spiffy, but she wasn't actually ill. Not yet, anyway.

When she reentered the office and found Tim gone she couldn't decide whether or not to be glad. She supposed she ought to be thankful, since his absence meant less conflict. But she also missed him; all six, tall-dark-and-handsome feet of him. Even when he was acting grumpy she wanted to be around him. Maybe not to talk to him directly, but to know he was there. That was crazy, she knew. It was also brutally honest as well as pretty scary.

Circling her desk, Dawn checked for messages before getting back to the reports she'd been typing. Except for calls from a couple of hopeful salesmen there was nothing pending. Good. That would give her more time in which to try to sort out her confusion.

Some of Gabi's advice had been valid, Dawn knew, yet she couldn't stop assuming that Tim had purposely dismissed the importance of her Christian practices. It wasn't excuse enough that Nora thought her son was simply reticent. It was much more than that.

The question was, did Dawn want to confront Tim about it and chance making things worse, or should she simply let the matter drop? If she forced the issue and Tim actually expressed disdain for her faith, would she be able to continue working for him or would she see him in such a negative light that she would be eventually forced to quit her job? That was the true crux of her dilemma. Logically, she was probably better off not knowing how he felt.

She was about to return the salesmen's calls when the office door burst open and Ada Smith entered on Tim's arm.

"Looky who I found downstairs!" Ada announced. "He showed up just in time, too. Those gargoyles in the lobby were about to throw me out, sure as the world."

"Louise and Herman Gordon are practically part of the furniture around here," Tim explained, avoiding eye-contact with Dawn. "They mean well. And they do a wonderful job of protecting us and keeping track of our staff."

Ada beamed up at him. "Well, if you say so."

Dawn had never seen the prim old woman look so radiant. Apparently, the effects of Tim Hamilton's charisma were not limited to ladies of his own generation.

Dawn smiled. "Hello, Ada. What brings you to Hamilton Media?"

"You do, dear. Don't you remember? You said you were going to tell my story just like you did that Stuart Meyers." She displayed a sly grin. "After I read what a wonderful job you did tellin' his story, I phoned him up and asked him what I needed to bring."

"You called Stuart?"

"Sure did. Nice fella, too, for an old codger."

That comment widened Dawn's smile. "Old codger?"

"Well, maybe not *that* old," Ada recanted. "Anyways, he told me to bring lots of pictures, so I did." Pointing at the shopping bag in Tim's opposite hand she said, "You can put 'em on our Dawn's desk, son. Much obliged for totin' 'em up here for me."

He did as he was told, then turned away. Dawn thought he might make it all the way into his office without deigning to look at her but she was mistaken. He gave her a parting glance at the very last second and unfortunately caught her staring right at him.

Mouth agape, she blinked rapidly, hoping to hide her reaction to his intensely poignant gaze. The floor tilted. Air drained out of the room till she couldn't catch her breath and she wondered why the windowpanes weren't being sucked in by the sudden vacuum.

Dawn knew the only thing that was really about to implode was her. That conclusion, however, didn't make it any easier to overcome her shaky equilibrium. The unreadable look in Tim's eyes had caught her gaze and was holding it fast, as if they were bound together by a powerful, invisible force.

Finally, he broke the contact, stepped into his office and drew the door closed behind him.

Ada began fanning herself with her hand. "Hoo-whee! That was enough to give me the vapors."

"I don't know what you're talking about."

"Shame on you. A good Christian girl like you ain't supposed to lie. I may be old but I ain't blind. You and that boy had this here air cracklin'!"

"You're imagining things."

"Hah!" The older woman wasn't about to be deterred. "I know that deer-in-the-headlights look of yours. Ought to. I've seen it often enough. And he wasn't no better. I ain't seen that many sparks fly since Papa Smith, God rest his soul, got the tail end of his chin whiskers caught in the 'lectric fence charger. It like to killed him afore he got himself loose!"

"Now that would make a good addition to our article about your life, especially if it's true," Dawn said. She picked up a pencil and poised it over a lined notepad. "Have a seat and tell me all about it. When did it happen?"

Ada plopped into the chair beside Dawn's desk

but her interest was not in herself. "I could be wrong. But if I am, it'll be the first time," she quipped. "I imagine one smile from Mr. Tim makes your pretty blue eyes twinkle like a lovesick firefly at the dark of the moon."

"I wouldn't know," Dawn said. "I've never seen a lovesick firefly."

"Then you ain't looked in any mirrors lately," Ada said with conviction. "'Cause if you had, you'd see it plain as day. You're in love, girl."

Dawn's vision clouded with unshed tears and she blinked them back. *Not again.* And not here where Tim might walk in and see her. *Please, God. Don't let me cry again.*

Ada reached over and patted her hand. "There, there. Don't you fret, honey. I been through lotsa heartbreaks in my time and let me tell you, every single one of 'em was well worth the tears."

"I don't know what you mean."

"I don't reckon you do or you wouldn't be so sad." She grinned and changed the subject. "Let's talk about me for a bit, shall we? I was borned in a little cabin up in the hills. My ma was a teacher till she married Pa and the school board made her quit." Pausing, Ada sniggered. "Didn't know they did that to women, did ya? Well, they did. Yes, sir. The only ones deemed fit to teach younguns were single girls—and a few men, married or not. Ma got mad every time she told that story. It galled her something fierce."

"I'm sure it did."

"There was a lot of good in the good old days but there was a lot of bad, too. Those of us that re- members can tell ya all about it. It's gettin' young folks to listen that's the hard part. That's why I think it's so good you're writin' our stories. So does Stuart."

Dawn smiled sweetly. "It's my pleasure."

"How come you got this job, anyways?"

"It was Mr. Hamilton's idea." Unbidden, Dawn's glance darted to his closed door for a split second.

"Good. Shows he thinks highly of you in more ways than one," Ada remarked. "Now, gettin' back to my ma. She used to tutor the neighbor's kids at our kitchen table. That's how I met my Sidney. He was a big ol' rough farm boy, as sweet as they come. His pa didn't take with schoolin' but his ma knew how important it was. She used to send him over to our place to deliver eggs and he'd stay for a lesson."

Ada chuckled low as she immersed herself in fond memories. "To this day I can hardly look at a fried egg. We sure ate a lot of 'em in those days. But it was worth it. Sid learned to read and I got me a good, hardworkin' husband."

She shook off the aura of pleasant remembrances to grin at Dawn. "Ain't too many of those left, you know. Good men, I mean. I think you've found yourself one, though."

Dawn knew exactly what she was getting at but chose to pretend otherwise. "I'm afraid you're mistaken, Miss Ada. There's no man in my life."

That seemed to really tickle the elderly woman

and she quoted, "'The lady doth protest too much methinks.'"

Dawn's pencil stilled. She stared. "Shakespeare?"

Ada cackled. "Hamlet. Act 3, scene 2, if I remember rightly. I told you my ma was an educated woman. Just because I choose to talk like a hillbilly most of the time doesn't mean there's no culture between my ears."

"Yes, ma'am."

She lowered her voice, leaned closer and spoke beside a cupped hand. "But if you blow my cover, as they say on those cop shows on TV, I'll deny every word of it."

Dawn laughed and made another note on the pad. "It'll be our secret. I promise."

"Good. Now that you know how smart I am, suppose you listen to my advice and give that poor man's broken heart a little more consideration."

"His heart's not broken," Dawn argued. "He's just miffed because I wouldn't skip church to go out with him."

"You sure about that?"

Dawn's lips pressed into a thin line and she nodded. "I'm positive."

Tim couldn't believe he'd misread the signals from Dawn. That kind of thing never happened to him in business. If he couldn't have sensed what a colleague or competitor was thinking he'd never have gotten this far in the corporate world. Then again, few of his business dealings were with young, beautiful women so he didn't have a broad sampling by which to judge. Perhaps that was the problem.

Most women liked him. He was sure of that. And he found them pleasant, if unpredictable, company. Dawn Leroux, however, was a special case. To say she was unlike the others was to greatly oversimplify a complex problem.

What he wanted to do was confront Dawn and insist she tell him where he'd gone wrong. He wouldn't do it, of course. A man had his pride. Still, it would be nice to know why she'd turned him down so forcefully and stormed out of the office when all she'd have had to do was say "no" and leave it at that.

The outer office was quiet. Tim decided to ease the door open and peek out to see if Ada had gone. She had. So had Dawn. He realized he'd been holding his breath and released it with a whoosh as he fully opened the door. He didn't intend to hide in his office and wait for his assistant to get over being mad at him but he wasn't looking forward to facing her, either. If anyone had asked him about such idiotic fears before, he'd have insisted nothing fazed him. Now, he wasn't so sure.

Crossing to her desk he noted that her computer was still on, signifying an intent to return. Good. At least she hadn't run off again. He picked up the yellow legal pad she'd been using to take notes during Ada's interview. The crowded, disorganized page looked as if her pencil had run amok. There didn't seem to be one coherent thought in the whole scratched-up mess.

Suddenly, Dawn burst in from the hallway. She froze, staring at the pad in his hand and making him feel like a nosy parent caught reading a child's diary. He flung the paper aside and it landed atop a short stack of unfinished work. "I wondered where you'd gone."

"I was walking Ada to her car," Dawn said crisply. She circled the desk and immediately slid the pad into her top drawer. "Was there something you needed?"

An explanation would be nice, Tim thought. Instead of asking for one he merely said, "No. Nothing."

She sat. "Well, then…?"

Realizing he'd just been dismissed from his own office, Tim set his jaw. Lately, he'd done a lot of things for which he was sorry, including feuding with his eldest brother, Jeremy. But their argument paled compared to the mistake he'd made when he'd asked his executive assistant for a date. Tim wished he could take back his invitation to the golf tourney and forget he'd ever considered including Dawn in his life. More than that, he wished she would forget he'd asked her.

Unfortunately, wishing one could change the past was a poor substitute for using common sense in the first place. He was stuck with the result of his social error and he knew it. The best he could hope for at the moment was a return of Dawn's former good humor. Failing that, he'd settle for a temporary truce. Anything was better than the charged atmosphere between them right now.

Turning on his heel, Tim went back into his office, slamming the door behind him. He hadn't intended to shove it closed quite that hard but now that he had, he had to admit the hard clap of wood against wood had made him feel better.

Dawn was getting pretty sick of feeling pretty sick. Off balance was a more apt description. When she'd seen Tim looking at her notes she'd wanted the floor to open up and swallow her.

She eased open the drawer and glanced down at the scribbled notes on the top sheet. Tim's name stood out like an alligator hunter's spotlight in a dark swamp. He apparently hadn't noticed her telltale doodling between the lines or surely he'd have commented.

"Thank You, Lord," Dawn whispered. "All I'd need is for him to see that. He'd think I was acting like a lovesick teenager!"

Which was exactly how she felt, Dawn realized with chagrin. Here she was, pushing thirty, and still fighting the same stupid emotions she'd battled in her teens. Terrific. Well, what was, was. It couldn't be helped. It could, however, be hidden. Nobody, least of all Tim Hamilton, was going to know how miserable she felt.

She was going to focus on being the exemplary Christian she'd been in the past—if it killed her.

And in the meantime, she was also going to reclaim the life she'd made for herself, starting with her comfortably old car. If the garage wasn't finished patching it up she'd haunt their establishment until they rushed the job just to get rid of her.

Standing by her desk, Dawn considered leaving a note so Tim would know where she'd gone, then decided not to. Nothing on her schedule was pressing. If she didn't get back to the office before quitting time she'd simply make up for her absence by coming in early or staying after hours, whatever was necessary to avoid running into Tim.

She sighed. The saddest part of all this was losing her joy about coming to work. Yes, she'd keep doing her best. And yes, she'd stay at Hamilton Media as long as they wanted her. But her elation about being there had vanished like the fog over a swamp in the sunshine of midday.

That was exactly the right analogy, Dawn mused. The light of truth had erased the lovely clouds of fantasy that had kept her from seeing Tim Hamilton's true character.

She supposed she should be praying and thanking her heavenly Father for that strikingly clear illumination but she just couldn't make herself pray that prayer. *Not yet. Not yet.* She swallowed hard. *Maybe never.*

Heather was downstairs in the lobby, apparently waiting for Dawn, when she arrived at the office several days later. They signed Herman's log and headed for the elevator together.

"So, how have you been?" Heather asked brightly.

"Fine. You?"

"Just great. I do have one little problem you may be able to help me with, though."

"Sure." Dawn pushed the button for the second floor for Heather and the third for herself. "What is it? Do you want to borrow the blue dress?"

"No." The other woman leaned against the richly paneled elevator wall and folded her arms across her chest. "I want you to tell me what's wrong with my brother."

"Who, Tim? How would I know?"

"You're the one most likely to know," Heather countered. "You see him far more than anyone else does. So why is he acting like he's just lost his best friend and his dog has been run over by a bus."

"I have no idea what you mean." Dawn frowned. "Wait a sec. What dog? Tim told me he's never had a pet."

"I was being facetious."

"Oh." She shrugged. "Well, maybe worrying about your father has made him tense. I mean, Wallace has been in and out of the hospital a lot lately."

"That's true. Has Tim gone with you to deliver meals-on-wheels again?"

"No."

"Have you invited him to?"

Dawn had to make a great effort to school her

features so they wouldn't give away too much
emotion. "He's a busy man. He has plenty to keep him
occupied without traipsing all over town with me."

"I suppose you're right."

"Of course I am. Maybe he's worried about the
business. He gets pretty uptight when things don't
run smoothly."

"I know. I looked into all that. Ed Bradshaw's
sure the paper is doing well and Amy says magazine
subscriptions are up, so it can't be that."

"Then I'm afraid I can't help you." They'd
reached Heather's floor. Dawn pressed her thumb
to the button that kept the door from closing.

"How are *you* doing?" Heather asked before
exiting. "Really."

"I'm fine. Just peachy. Righter than rain." Her
bottom lip began to quiver.

Heather touched her shoulder in a gesture of camaraderie and consolation before stepping into the
hall. "That's what I thought. Hang in there, okay?
Whatever's bugging Tim can't last forever. He'll get
over it and things will be back to normal soon. I
know they will."

Deeply touched, all Dawn could do was nod.
She saw the other woman wave as the brass doors
whooshed shut.

The elevator began to rise. Overcome with
emotion and knowing she was about to lose control,
Dawn pushed the red button for emergency stop.
The car jolted to a halt between floors and she
buried her face in her hands.

Tears came, unhindered, and in moments she was sobbing her heart out. With them came a revelation, a certainty she'd been denying ever since Tim had begun treating her with such disdain. She couldn't take much more, couldn't stay much longer. If something didn't happen soon to temper his ire she was going to have to start looking for another place to work. It was a coward's way out, she knew, yet she couldn't visualize herself weeping constantly until retirement!

That colorful insight was so vivid it tied her stomach in knots and settled there like a boulder.

Dawn waylaid Gabi after work and invited her out for coffee.

"Sorry," Gabi said, leading the way to the hospital parking lot. "I can't. I have to pick up the girls. Why don't you ride along? We can talk on the way."

"I suppose I could leave my car here and go with you. I finally got it back." She pointed. "Over there. See?"

"Hey! Nice. I like that color blue. It looks like the whole thing was painted."

"It was. Tim insisted on having it done."

"Good for him."

"Yeah, well…"

Gabi snickered. "That poor man couldn't please you right now if he bought you that fancy loaner you've been cruising around in for the past few weeks. What's wrong with you, anyway?"

"I don't know. That's what I wanted to talk to you about."

Leading the way to her car, Gabi unlocked it and slid behind the wheel. "Okay. Talk."

Dawn plopped into the passenger's seat and sighed as she fastened her seat belt. "I wondered if you might know of a job opening at the hospital."

"For who? For you? That's ridiculous. You have a wonderful job at Hamilton Media."

"It *was* wonderful," Dawn countered. "Past tense."

The pretty Latina rolled her eyes and shook her head slowly. "Now I've heard everything. You have to be nuts, girl. Why would you want to leave a perfectly good executive position for an entry-level job in this hospital?" Before Dawn could answer she continued, "And don't tell me it's because Tim Hamilton is a snake in the grass because we both know he's not. He may not be one hundred percent ideal but he's not so bad you have to quit working for him."

"Who says?"

"I do! If you can't think clearly, somebody had better do it for you."

"There's nothing unclear about how I feel," Dawn argued.

"Maybe not. But there are sure a lot of problems with how you're dealing with those feelings. We can't pick and choose which parts of the Scriptures we follow, you know. What about forgiveness and tolerance?" She raised an eyebrow. "What about everybody being equal in God's eyes. Do you think you're more equal than Tim Hamilton is?"

"Of course not!"

"Well, that's how it looks to me, kiddo."

Subdued by the realization her friend could be right, Dawn stared out the window at the passing scenery, seeing little. Did she think she was somehow better than Tim because she was a practicing Christian? Apparently. Which meant she was anything but better. If acknowledging God's magnificent grace in her own life didn't bring at least a measure of humility she was definitely missing the point.

"I have to stay where I am, don't I?" Dawn asked, already knowing the answer.

"That's up to you," Gabi said wisely, "but it sure looks that way to me. When you've had a chance to cool off and think more clearly, you'll see what's right."

"I hope so." She blinked to clear her misty vision. "I just wish…"

"Have you prayed about it?" Gabi asked.

"Of course I…well…maybe not as **much** as I should have."

"Why is that?"

Dawn huffed and made a face. "Why? Honestly? I suppose because I didn't want to give the problem to God and take the chance I'd get a solution I didn't like."

Chuckling softly, her friend nodded. "I think you're finally beginning to understand."

"Understand? Yeah, right. That doesn't make it any easier to face Tim every day."

"Hey, who promised this Christian walk was

going to be easy? When Octavio died I thought my life was over, and now look at me."

Dawn was contrite. "You're right. Compared to all you've been through, my problems are stupid."

"I didn't say that. All I meant was, we each have our own crosses to bear. Some look heavier than others, that's all. It's when things are the most difficult for us that we most often tend to stop and look up. In retrospect, it's easier to see how God stayed right beside us, even in the toughest times. I think that's why mature Christians seem to take setbacks more in stride, no matter how badly they hurt."

Dawn nodded. "You're right. Instead of complaining, I guess I should be thanking my heavenly Father for giving me such an inconsequential problem."

That observation made her friend laugh out loud. "Love is never inconsequential, honey. Confusing and maddening, maybe, but never inconsequential."

Chapter Fourteen

The monthly Hamilton family dinner was a long-standing tradition that Nora had insisted on maintaining, even while Wallace was in the hospital. Tim dreaded going, yet he knew how important each family gathering was to his mother so he didn't even consider begging off.

It would be good to spend some quality time with Chris, Tim thought. They ran into each other infrequently in the course of their busy lives, especially since Chris had solved the mystery of Felicity's stalker and had quit spending so much time hanging around the newspaper office, working on the case.

Heather and Amy would undoubtedly be in attendance, complete with their partners, and Chris would bring Felicity if he wasn't on duty. Tim hoped his mother wouldn't nag too much about his own lack of companionship. He knew she meant well but he was getting pretty sick of hearing about how happy all his siblings were, with the exception of the missing ones, of course.

It was hard for Tim to keep from gritting his teeth as he climbed the familiar front steps onto the porch. Thoughts of Jeremy always did that to him, not to mention those of Melissa. The oldest and the youngest; still missing and still breaking their mother's heart. Didn't they know what their prolonged absences were doing to her? Didn't they care? Apparently not.

Tim rapped on the heavy, glass-inlaid front door as he pushed it open and called, "Mom? I'm here."

From the back of the house came a gaggle of voices, some laughing, some calling greetings. Tim winced. Every one of them sounded a hundred percent happier than he was—and he'd been doing his best to cultivate a carefree persona.

At that moment, he would have turned and left if a sense of duty hadn't held him there.

Amy was the first to bustle through the doorway from the dining room. She greeted him with a brief hug and a grin. "Congratulations, Tim. You got here in time for the first course this month."

"I'm glad to see you, too," he said with a smirk. "And I wasn't that late last time. I was here before Vera Mae brought the food out of the kitchen."

"Barely." Amy laughed. She motioned to the man and boy lagging behind her. They were dressed in slacks and matching sweaters as if one was a carbon copy of the other. "You know Bryan. And this is his son, Dylan."

"Of course. Hello, Bryan." Tim shook the hand of the slightly shorter, auburn-haired writer who had recently been added to the magazine staff. "My sister tells me you're full of good ideas."

"Tim!"

One look at Amy told him she'd mistaken his innocent compliment for an allusion to her romantic involvement with the man. He laughed and quickly added, "I meant story ideas for *Nashville Living*."

Bryan chuckled. "Nice save, Tim." He stepped aside so Dylan couldn't hide behind his leg as easily. "Say hello to Mr. Hamilton, son."

The five-year-old seemed shy so Tim crouched to his level and extended his hand. "Hi, Dylan. You can call me Uncle Tim, okay?"

"'Kay."

Blinking behind his glasses, the freckle-faced child extended his hand to shake with Tim the way his father had. Tim treated the boy with decorum equal to that of a business acquaintance, shook his small hand, then straightened. "Glad to see you two here. It'll do Mom good to have a youngster in the house again."

"That's what Amy said," Bryan told him. "We didn't want to intrude but she assured me we'd be welcome."

"That, you are. Where's everybody else?"

"Last I saw, Ethan was going to take pictures of Heather in the garden by the terrace. He said something about getting shots of her by the crape myrtle while it was still in bloom. Chris and Felicity are with them. There was so much talk about weddings I made myself scarce." His quiet laugh was cut short as Amy whapped him playfully on the arm.

Tim couldn't remember when he'd seen his sister glow with such contentment. It was enough to turn a man's stomach. What was wrong with all these people? Didn't they know Wallace might die? Didn't they worry about anyone else's future the way he did?

Tim felt a small, warm hand slip into his, looked down and saw the little boy smiling up at him. His eyes were twinkling, framed behind the lenses of his glasses. Dylan was the only one in that house who could be truly carefree, wasn't he? And that was only because he was too young to understand how difficult life could be.

The instant he drew that erroneous conclusion, Tim was regretful. The poor kid had lost his mother before he'd even known her. At least the Hamilton children had grown up in a secure home with two parents who loved them. And now it looked as though Amy would be giving this motherless child the love he'd been missing all his short life. That poignant thought was almost enough to choke Tim up.

Dylan tugged on his hand as Bryan and Amy left them and started back to rejoin the others. "Uncle Tim?"

"Yes?"

"Do you have kids like my Uncle Kevin in Texas?"

"Nope. Sorry."

"Oh, well. Will you play with me?"

"Me? Sure, I guess so. What do you want to play?"

"Do you have any toys?"

"I'm afraid not. Not anymore."

The boy's face fell. "Oh."

"But maybe we can find something fun to do before dinner. Come on." He led the child through the doorway into the entry. "We could play hide-and-seek."

"That's no fair. You know all the good places to hide and I don't."

"I wish I had some of those toy soldiers I gave Mr. Meyers. Maybe someday I'll take you to meet him and you can play with his plastic men. He's got a whole army. Actually, two armies."

"Cool." Another tug. The child pointed. "Uncle Tim? Did you ever slide down that thing?"

"The staircase? Sure. I rode that banister lots of times when my mother wasn't looking."

"Really?" There was more awe in the question than Tim had heard in ages. "Can I do it? Please?"

"I don't know. I wouldn't want you to get hurt."

"You never did, did you?"

"No. And Chris wasn't any older than you are the first time Jeremy and I put him up there and gave him a push. Tell you what. I'll help you do it if you'll promise you won't try again unless I'm there to catch you. Promise?"

"Uh-huh."

He took a tentative step forward, holding tight to Tim's hand. "Will Grandma Nora be mad?"

An ear-splitting grin spread across Tim's face and he noticed how much more lighthearted he was becoming in the presence of this extraordinary child. "She'll be furious if she sees us," Tim said with a laugh. "But if we get in trouble, I'll take all the blame."

"You're a cool uncle," Dylan said.

"Well, you're a cool nephew, too, so I guess that makes us even." He led the way to the staircase and hefted the boy into his arms so he could place him a short distance up the curving banister. "Don't be afraid. I'll be right here to catch you."

"Okay!" Dylan leaned down, his stomach pressed against the rising wooden rail and held on.

Tim released him, encircling him with his arms so he wouldn't fall even if he lost his balance. Nothing happened. "You can't grab it quite that tight or you won't go anywhere," Tim said. "Loosen up a little."

Trembling, the boy eased his grip. Sliding slowly, he descended the few feet to the base of the stairs and came to a stop where the carved wood formed a tight spiral. His eyes were wide with delight when he looked up at Tim.

"Can I do it again?"

"Sure, sport, but you'd better let me hold your glasses for you this time, just in case."

"Okay." He scampered up the stairs, going farther than the first time. Pausing, he carefully removed his glasses and handed them to Tim, then held out his arms to be picked up again.

The sight of the trusting, eager child tugged at Tim's heart. He'd never had much to do with kids before, but this one was sure getting under his skin. He could picture his own childhood and little glimmers of remembrance kept darting into his consciousness. There had been fun times then, carefree hours spent in this very house in the company of his siblings. Melissa, Jeremy, Chris and Heather had usually been the instigators of any trouble they'd gotten into, while he and Amy had stood back and thought things through. Especially him, Tim conceded. He'd been the sensible one of the bunch. The cautious one.

So what was he doing helping a five-year-old slide down a banister? Was he crazy? Even if Dylan repeated the slide a hundred times and never got hurt there was always the chance he might lose his balance and fall.

"Listen, kid," Tim said. "I've been thinking. Maybe this isn't such a good idea after all."

"Aww. You promised."

Tim sighed. "I did, didn't I? Okay. One more time and then we stop."

"But—"

"No arguments. Once more is it."

"Okay." The pout was replaced with a sheepish grin. "You're harder to talk into doing stuff than Dad is."

"Am I?" The candid comment made Tim smile, too. "I'm not surprised. That's what my brothers and sisters always used to say, too."

"You have brothers and sisters? Where?"

"All over the place. Amy's my sister."

"No way! She's *old.*"

Tim was still laughing to himself over that innocent remark when he led Dylan into the dining room to join the others for dinner.

Vera Mae had once again volunteered to help with the monthly family get-together. She had already served the main course when the telephone rang. She answered it in the kitchen, then quickly brought the portable receiver to Nora.

"It's Mr. Jeremy," the longtime maid said. "I thought you'd want to take it now, even if it does interrupt your meal."

No one else spoke. Tim saw his mother's hand shaking as she lifted the instrument to her ear and said, "Hello?"

She listened. Tears filled her eyes and she glanced at Wallace's empty chair at the head of the table. "Yes, he's much better. The doctors think he'll be released from the hospital soon."

She looked around at her other children, smiled and nodded reassuringly. "Yes, Jeremy. Everybody's here except Melissa. Do you want me to put this on speaker so they can hear, too?"

His answer must have been in the affirmative because Nora held out the phone and pushed the button to let the rest of them in on the conversation. "Okay. Go ahead and tell us. We're all listening," she said.

Tim was more relieved to hear his brother's voice than he'd imagined he'd be. He tensed, however, when he heard, "I've found my paternal grandparents, Thelma and Chester Anderson, here in Florida. Like we thought, they had no clue they had a grandson."

When he paused, Nora asked, "How are they taking it?"

"Fairly well, considering. Thelma's pretty open to the idea. I can understand why my father left and didn't tell them anything about where he was going or what he was doing, though. Chester's a hard man." There was a drawn-out, noisy sigh. "Tell…Wallace…I'm really thankful I grew up where I did, okay? I'd hate to be a kid and have to face a guy like Chester. It's difficult enough having to deal with him now."

"You're coming home soon?" Nora asked.

There was a long pause. Tim clenched his fists.

"Not right away," Jeremy said. "I want to give this a chance. It's a big adjustment for everybody and like I said, Thelma's a really nice lady. She says my blue eyes look just like her son Paul's did."

That was more than Tim could stand. "You might want to think more about the man who raised you and gave you everything," he announced.

"I am thinking of Wallace," Jeremy replied. "He's the one who taught me to do what I believed was right, and that's exactly what I'm doing. I had to do this, Tim. I don't see that I had much of a choice, considering."

"Of course you had to find them," Nora said with a cautionary glance toward her second son. "Tim worries too much. We know you'd be back here if you could. Just take care of yourself and come home as soon as you can. We all miss you."

"I miss you all, too. Bye for now. I'll call again soon and give you an update, I promise."

From around the table there was a chorus of shouted goodbyes. Even Tim responded without urging.

Nora blinked back tears, said, "I love you, Jeremy," then pushed the button to end their conversation.

For long seconds, no one spoke. Then, Dylan piped up with a cheery, "I ate all my peas. Can I have dessert now?" and everyone resumed as normal a demeanor as was possible under the strained circumstances.

Amy looked across at her brother. "Nice one, *Timmy*. You almost blew it."

He grimaced at the childhood put-down. Amy hadn't called him "Timmy" in at least twenty-five years. "Yeah, I know. Sorry," he grumbled.

His sister merely rolled her eyes and said no more but Tim could tell everyone was upset with him. Truth to tell, he was pretty upset with himself, too.

The longer Tim sat at the enormous dining table and looked at his assembled family members, the more isolated he felt. As ridiculous and illogical as it was, he was so lonesome he felt as if he were the only person in the whole world, let alone the dining room.

Visions of Dawn kept nagging at his subconscious. She understood him better than anyone else and she wasn't speaking to him, either, although in her case he had no earthly notion why.

Like it or not, Dawn was in everything he thought about; as much a part of him as the bricks were a part of the house in which he sat. What had gone wrong between them? He and Dawn had seemed as if they were really growing closer, getting to know each other, and then she'd pulled away as though she'd suddenly discovered he was a dangerous fugitive or something equally as ridiculous.

There had to be a sensible explanation for her actions. Even *women* had reasons for behaving the way they did, didn't they? Not knowing what had so radically changed her opinion of him was the most bothersome. Facts, he could deal with. Suppositions left him in limbo.

Finally, Tim excused himself from the table and stepped into the hallway on the pretext he needed to make a private call on his cell phone.

Hesitating, he stared at the instrument. If he asked Dawn to join him tonight and she turned him down, he'd be no better off than before. Then again, if he didn't make the call things would stay the same. That was unacceptable. His only logical recourse was to take the chance, call her and let God handle the details. After the disappointment of his apparently ignored prayers for his father's renewed health, that spiritually based conclusion caught him off guard.

Tim dialed. The tone stopped abruptly after four rings and he was afraid he'd gotten Dawn's answering machine until he heard her breathless, "Hello?"

"Dawn? Tim Hamilton." He cleared his throat. "I hate to bother you on a Sunday afternoon. I'm over at Mom and Dad's." A brilliant idea popped into his head so abruptly he voiced it without further consideration. Happily, it was also based in truth. "We've been discussing an acquisition and I need to see the Peterson file."

"You need it *now?* Why?"

"I just do. Can you get it to me before six?"

"What happens at six?"

"Some of us are going over to the hospital to visit Dad and I wanted to take it with me."

"I suppose I could drop it by the hospital on my way to church."

Tim was exasperated. "No. I need it before that. Please bring it to the house. You know where it is, right?"

"The house or the file?"

"Both."

"Yes, I know. I was there recently with Heather, remember?"

How could he forget? Images of Dawn in that beautiful blue dress still kept him awake nights. He schooled his voice to hide any telltale emotion. "Good. I'll look forward to seeing you. Thanks. Bye."

Just before he broke the connection he was certain he heard her mumbling. Thankfully, she was too polite to voice her negative opinion of him clearly and he hoped she'd have calmed down by the time she arrived. If not, maybe he'd made things worse.

Tim snorted in self-derision. If his unreasonable request did result in an argument, at least they'd be speaking to each other, which was a distinct improvement over their recent lack of communication. It was hard to run Hamilton Media when your executive assistant refused to say more than two words to you.

More anxious about Dawn's imminent arrival than he'd dreamed he'd be, Tim went outside to pace the drive and wait for her. He knew he'd be the brunt of plenty of jokes if anyone noticed his unusual behavior but he didn't care. He was going to be right there to greet her, to welcome her warmly the minute she pulled into the driveway.

And he wasn't going to let her leave until they'd talked and she'd told him what had gone so wrong.

Chapter Fifteen

Dawn had held a fruitless dialogue with herself all the way from Hickory Mills to Davis Landing. What had gotten into her boss? He might choose to work overtime himself but he'd never before asked her to return to the office on one of her days off.

She'd found the file Tim had requested and had briefly leafed through it in the elevator on her way back down to the ground floor.

He must have finally worked his brain into a hopeless knot, she decided as she tossed the folder onto the front seat, climbed into her car and hit the road. There was so little information on those few pages she could just as easily have read the Peterson file to him over the telephone.

The notion of calling him back and doing just that appealed to her, yet she knew Tim too well to try. If he said he wanted the actual file, he wanted the actual file. Period. Being flexible was not one of his virtues. If the day ever came that Tim Hamilton took things in stride, everybody who worked for him would probably faint dead away.

That silly thought made Dawn smile. Poor man. He obviously had no idea how unreasonable his attitudes appeared to others, or how much happier he'd be if he loosened up a little and led a less regimented life.

Then again, she admitted ruefully, she was pretty set in her ways, too, which was why she'd better hurry. If she didn't complete her errand for Tim in a timely manner and get back to Northside ASAP, she was going to be late for Sunday evening services.

Pulling into the driveway of the Hamilton house she noted the glut of cars. Felicity's '59 Caddy was parked next to a motorcycle that was undoubtedly Chris Hamilton's. Heather's sporty Saab was missing, probably because she'd ridden over with Ethan in his SUV, but Amy's Camry was present, as well as Tim's familiar BMW and a few other models she didn't recognize. The eclectic group of vehicles reminded her of an upscale used car lot! Either that or there was a dandy party going on inside.

Tim's BMW was the last in line so Dawn stopped her car behind it. To her surprise, Tim appeared and quickly jogged over to her.

She rolled down her car window and held up the file. "Here you go."

Instead of taking it, Tim opened her door.

"Thanks. Won't you come in? We were about to have dessert."

She checked her watch. "I'm really pressed for time, Thanks, anyway."

He remained steadfast. "At least say hello."

Dawn pulled a face. "Hello. Now let go of my door."

"Sorry. I can't do that. You and I need to have a serious talk. It's high time we got a few things out in the open and aired our grievances."

"I have no grievances," she insisted, "except maybe having to run errands for you on a Sunday."

"Okay. We'll count that as number one. Let's take a walk around the grounds and discuss others."

"I can't. I'll be late." She saw how determined he was and felt an unusual tugging from her subconscious. "I have to get to church."

"Will it hurt you to miss once?" Tim asked.

That question pushed her angry button. Dawn bailed out of the car and confronted him with her hands fisted on her hips. "You just don't get it, do you? Being a Christian is important to me. It's what I do. Who I am."

"I understand that," Tim said softly. "I was brought up in church, too. But I sometimes wonder if God isn't sitting up there laughing at all the rituals and rigid rules men have devised to try to worship Him properly."

"You don't like church, do you? Never mind. You don't have to answer that. It's crystal clear how you feel. You don't value the faith you grew up with so you expect everybody else to treat their beliefs with the same kind of casual disdain. Well, I don't agree, okay?"

Tim's expression was one of astonishment. "What's gotten into you? You preach love and brotherhood but you're not willing to let anyone else have an opinion if it's not exactly the same as yours? What would Pastor Abernathy say?"

She opened her mouth to answer, then paused to give her brain time to catch up with her tongue. A simple truth from that morning's sermon kept nagging at her, insisting it be repeated. She'd never preached to Tim, never dreamed she'd want to, but this particular analogy needed to be passed along. Now. Whether or not she felt ready to do so.

"Funny you should ask. Okay, fine. We'll talk." Turning from the car she started to walk toward a garden path that looked as though it circled the massive old house. As she'd assumed he would, Tim followed.

As soon as they'd found a shady site and temporary privacy, she turned to him and said, "I know I can't explain this as well as Pastor Abernathy did but I'm going to try. Just bear with me. Please?"

"Of course." Tim directed her to a stone bench. "Let's sit here."

Dawn shook her head. "Uh-uh. I'm too nervous to sit still. I need to stand." She began to pace and gesture. "It's like this—faith isn't mental or intellectual, it's emotional and spiritual."

"Okay. I'm with you so far."

She managed a slight smile. "Good. Let's assume you're looking at Christianity the same way a man who is scared to fly looks at an airplane. Intellectually, he knows that flying is safer than traveling by car but emotionally he can't convince himself to actually take a chance and get on board. He's heard all about what an airliner does. He's watched lots of them pass overhead. He knows planes fly. He believes in flight. But until he actually gets on that plane and it takes off, he isn't investing any real faith in the process."

"What are you talking about? I know planes can fly."

"This is symbolic, not literal," she said, getting more frustrated by the second. "It's about absolute trust. What it means is, you can't be a Christian by standing on the outside looking in and hoping you'll someday understand it all. Millions of people believe in Jesus with their heads. The key is to open your heart and place all your trust *on* Him, just like the man who finally climbed on board that hypothetical airplane. Unless you give your faith a chance like that, you'll never really see how far it can take you." She snapped her fingers. "If you don't, you could miss Heaven by that much."

"You selling plane tickets? Is that it?"

Dawn gave a self-deprecating laugh. "Me? I'm barely hanging on by my fingernails in the baggage compartment. I imagine Pastor Abernathy would be delighted to help you book your flight, though."

"If I talked to him, would that satisfy you?"

"I'm not the one you need to please, Tim. God is."

"I know, but you're the one who's been giving me the cold shoulder lately. Would you care to explain what that's been about?" He smiled slightly. "And keep it simple, okay? No more fancy airplane stories. Just tell it like it is."

Dawn was flabbergasted. Her jaw dropped. "You really don't know?"

"Not a clue." He raked his fingers through his hair and shook his head. "Honest."

She believed him. He looked far too confused to be anything but sincerely baffled. "Oh, dear. I guess I owe you an apology then."

"I'd gladly settle for an explanation."

"It was the Sunday golf tournament," Dawn said. "You acted like it shouldn't matter to me what day it fell on so I assumed you were disregarding the importance of my church commitment."

"You thought I didn't care?"

"Exactly."

"Why didn't you *say* so?"

"I don't know. My friend Gabi asked me the same thing. Let me ask you a question. If you had suggested we go somewhere on a Monday or Wednesday night and I'd said I couldn't, would you have assumed I was being difficult or would you have remembered the meals-on-wheels deliveries?"

"I suppose I'd have remembered the deliveries."

"Right. Because you think they're important."

"And because I ran the route with you. I am beginning to see your point, though." A smile was teasing at the corners of his mouth, threatening to widen. "So, you weren't turning me down because you hate my guts?"

"Of course not!"

"That's a big relief." The smile became a grin. "Where do we go from here?"

She looked at him quizzically. "Go?"

"Sure. I'd only invited you to the golf tournament because I wanted to see if we had a chance as a couple. What do you think? Do we?"

"A couple? Us?"

Tim laughed quietly. "Yes, Ms. Leroux. A couple. If we were kids I'd ask you to go steady. Since we're past that stage, I guess we'll have to just call it an understanding. I'd like to start seeing more of you, dating you, if that's all right."

He grasped her hands and held them tenderly. "All I ask is that you tell me when—if—I make another mistake, instead of getting mad and ignoring me. Think you can do that?"

All she could manage was a silent nod. Happy tears threatened.

Tim put one finger under her chin to urge her to lift her face to his, then bent and placed a kiss on her trembling lips.

Dawn slid her arms around his waist and closed her eyes. A single tear escaped to glide down her cheek.

As Tim gently kissed the tear away she knew her prayers had been answered in a manner that would someday carry them far beyond her fondest dreams.

* * *

Church the following Sunday was extra special for Dawn because Tim was beside her. She'd even asked for a substitute to teach her Sunday school class so she could devote all her attention to introducing him and making him feel welcome.

Pastor Charles David Abernathy greeted them at the door to the sanctuary with a firm grip and a smile on his freckled face that left no doubt how happy he was to note their mutual arrival.

"Dawn! And Tim Hamilton! What a wonderful surprise. It's great to see you." He gave Tim's hand a hearty shake. "Got you with our food, did we? Those potlucks work every time."

Tim laughed and pumped the pastor's hand. "A lot of things contributed. Dawn repeated that airplane story of yours and got me to thinking."

"Wonderful!" He directed a brief wink in Dawn's direction. "I work hard on my sermons. It's good to hear that somebody's paying attention."

She laughed lightly. "I'm afraid it may have lost a lot in the retelling but I did my best."

"That's all the Lord asks of us," Charles David said. He looked to Tim. "If you'd like to talk about it more, I'm always available."

"Thanks. I'll give you a call in a week or so."

"Good, good." Nodding, he stepped aside to greet the next arrivals and Dawn led Tim down the center aisle.

"There's your mother and Heather in the third row," Dawn said. "Want to go sit with them?"

"Sure. Whatever."

"I want you to be comfortable."

"That may take a while. Being here on Sunday morning instead of teeing off at the country club still feels a little strange, but I suppose I'll eventually get used to it."

He hesitated and stopped her with a brief touch on her arm. "Hey, isn't that Stuart Meyers sitting over there?"

"Where?" Her eyes widened. "It sure is. And look who he's with! I've never seen Ada Smith here at Northside before."

"Well, well. I'm glad I asked her to write that grandmotherly advice column for the paper. Maybe we should start keeping track of how many people make new friends after they're featured in the *Dispatch*."

"No kidding. I love this. Look. They're waving. Aren't they cute together?"

"Not as cute as you and I are," Tim whispered aside. "I thought your pastor was going to split his cheeks grinning when we walked in."

"What can I say? He's a happy guy."

"So, am I," Tim said.

He took her arm gently and led her forward to where his family sat.

Dawn couldn't help grinning as broadly as Pastor Abernathy had when she said "Good morning" to Nora, Heather and Ethan and saw the astonishment on their faces. They scooted over to make room.

Felicity Simmons and Chris Hamilton soon

joined the group. Dawn couldn't help noticing that Felicity was wearing a sparkling diamond on the third finger of her left hand, especially since Felicity waggled her hand dramatically in front of their faces to display the new ring.

Tim stood and reached to shake his brother's hand while the women fussed over Felicity. "Congratulations, Chris."

"Thanks."

Heather leaned forward and smiled at her twin. "Good going, Chris. You never could stand it if I got ahead of you, could you?"

"I did get pretty tired of seeing you and Ethan acting so superior," Chris replied. "All we have to do now is decide which of us gets married first. I'd kind of wanted to wait till Dad was able to be part of the ceremony."

"Us, too," Heather said, patting Nora's thin hand. "It won't be long. I know it won't. He's looking better all the time."

Amy, Bryan and Dylan slipped into the pew behind Dawn and Tim. The minute Dylan spotted his new Uncle Tim he told his daddy he wanted to sit with him, instead.

"Not now, son," Bryan said. "After church we'll all go out to eat and you can sit with Tim then."

The child began to wiggle and whine.

Tim turned just as Bryan rose to carry his son out of the main sanctuary. "It's okay with me if you let him sit with us this morning," Tim said. "I owe him a lot."

"That's okay. He's better off with the other kids. But thanks anyway."

Puzzled, Dawn scowled at Tim as Bryan left. "You owe Dylan? What for?"

"For waking me up to what I might be missing if I didn't swallow my pride and call you."

"Let me guess. You didn't really need the Peterson file?"

"Nope."

"Whew! That's a relief. I was beginning to think you'd lost your mind."

Tim laced their fingers together. "It's my heart I've lost, not my mind. Love must be contagious. It looks like practically my whole family has caught the bug."

"Except for Jeremy and Melissa," Nora offered sadly.

Tim sobered and Dawn grasped his hand more tightly to express her support. Before she could decide what to say, music began to fill the sanctuary.

Dawn looked up and saw Gabi marching in with the choir. The minute their eyes met, the pretty Latina smiled and elbowed their mutual friend, Stella, who was standing next to her. Both women focused on Dawn and her companion, looking as if they were so overjoyed they could hardly contain their glee.

Dawn snuck a sidelong peek at Tim, hoping the undue attention wouldn't upset him. To her delight, he seemed to be taking everything in stride.

They were going to make it as a couple, she

decided with a rush of thankfulness. Their differences were not as strong as their affection for each other and with a little effort and the Lord's blessing, they were going to work things out.

Living happily-ever-after might not be without trials, but it was definitely doable.

The service seemed to fly by—even Pastor Abernathy's sermon. Dawn was so content sitting there beside Tim she hated to have to leave when everyone was dismissed after the closing prayer.

"Bryan and Amy want us to go to dinner with them," Tim said, escorting her up the center aisle while the other couple went to reclaim Dylan. "Is that all right with you?"

"Sure. The more the merrier."

"After we eat, I want to swing by your apartment."

That took her aback. "You do?"

"Uh-huh." He gave her a lopsided smile. "I stopped at the store and bought a peace offering for Beauregard and I'd like to give it to him myself."

"Okay, but I don't want you to be disappointed if he snubs it. He may look like he'd gladly eat a horse but he can be kind of fussy."

To her relief, Tim laughed and said, "Don't worry. I've got that covered."

"How?"

"You know me," he said. "How do you think?"

Dawn began to chuckle. "You bought a whole sackful of doggy treats?"

"Two sacks," Tim said. "I aim to please."

"If you really want to please, just be yourself and Beau and I will both be crazy about you."

"It can't be that easy," Tim countered.

She grasped his hand and held on tight. "Yes, it can. You don't have to buy your way into our affection. Money isn't everything, you know."

"I'm starting to see that," Tim said, looking around at the dispersing congregation. "These people seem to come from all walks of life, yet they're happy."

"That's right. They are."

"In a way, it's a relief you dislike money so much," Tim said. "That way, when I do ask you to marry me I won't have to buy you an expensive ring like Chris got for Felicity."

Dawn's head whipped around. "*Marry* me?"

"Yes. As soon as we're sure it's for keeps, I intend to do just that," he said. "I'm old-fashioned. I plan to get married only once."

Blushing, she nodded. "Okay. In that case it might be all right if you bought me a nice ring. But just *one*."

"One ring, one wife. What a concept," Tim teased. "Wait till I tell Dad about this partnership we're planning. It'll make his day."

Dawn laughed and squeezed his hand. "I don't doubt that. It's sure done wonders for mine!"

Epilogue

"Have you heard the latest?" he asked with a sneer. "Chris Hamilton is engaged to that *Dispatch* reporter he was guarding."

"Yeah. I saw them together at church this morning. She was waving around a rock the size of my thumbnail. I should be so lucky."

"Well, what are we going to do about it?" The man's face was reddening and contorting with anger.

"Nothing, unless you can come up with some more dirt on the Hamiltons," the woman answered. "I've done all I can. Even the *Observer* insists on some semblance of truth behind the stories I give them before they'll go to press."

"I did get an idea while I was at Betty's Bake-shoppe a while back," he said. "I couldn't hear everything that was being talked about but I know it involved the Hamiltons. Tim was there with that assistant of his and Betty seemed to get really upset.

I'll keep digging. Somebody will slip sooner or later and tell me something we can use."

She smiled cynically. "Good. Keep me posted. I hear the old man is getting better. It's high time we hit the family with another bombshell and gave them exactly what they deserve."

"I couldn't agree more," he said with a look of disdain. "I couldn't agree more."

* * * * *

Dear Reader,

Once again I have been asked to collaborate with five other authors to create my part of this ongoing story, which is book number four in the inspiring DAVIS LANDING series.

Many thanks to my fellow authors, Arlene, Kathryn, Irene, Patricia and Lenora, and to our editor, Diane, of course. We brainstormed via e-mail and worked hard to make our series books fit together, as well as be wonderful, stand-alone tales of love and faith.

In this book there is a lot of consideration given to whether it's important for believers to be involved in a local church. I think it is. It's been my experience, as we've moved around the country, that the most essential thing to look for when choosing a church is what's being taught inside. Churches are full of fallible people, just like me, so not one of them is perfect, but if you will seek out a place where the gospel of Jesus Christ is being preached, that will help you make the right choice.

I have been blessed to have found such a church here in Arkansas. Its pastor, Brother John, is an excellent teacher and true believer who leads by example, in and out of church, as well as by his words from the pulpit. It is a privilege to know him.

I love to hear from readers. The quickest replies are by e-mail—VALW@CENTURYTEL.NET—or you can write to me at P.O. Box 13, Glencoe, AR, 72539 and I'll do my best to answer as soon as I can. Or look at www.valeriehansen.com.

Blessings,

Valerie Hansen

QUESTIONS FOR DISCUSSION

1. Dawn questions why her prayers for her brother's total healing were apparently unanswered. If she were a more mature Christian who had had greater experience with God's wisdom, do you think she would still struggle? Do you struggle with something like that?

2. When Dawn is pushed beyond her comfort zone by being asked to write a feature article, she doubts her ability, then surprises herself by enjoying the task. Can work be a blessing, rather than a chore? Does it help to view it that way?

3. Dawn and Tim come from very different backgrounds. If Dawn has trouble relating to him, as he is, is she guilty of reverse discrimination? Why is it so hard for her to accept that his family has more monetary blessings? Should Tim be embarrassed by what the Lord has done for him?

4. Dawn is a community volunteer. She has no trouble giving of herself and is truly blessed to be able to help others, yet she has difficulty accepting help, especially from Tim. Why is that so much harder to do?

5. The older folks Dawn visits and later interviews have much to offer to younger people. Are there similar interesting individuals in your community? Do you know them?

6. Due to circumstances beyond her control, Dawn's life had not turned out the way she planned. Is that a bad thing? In retrospect, does she begin to understand that her path through life may be different than expected without being bad?

7. When Dawn is being coerced into letting Tim buy her a new outfit for the party, she resists. Do you think she was wrong to finally give in? Does accepting the fancy dress damage her reputation or hurt her Christian walk? What would you do in her place?

8. Tim comes from a large family. Dawn has only one brother. Setting aside the differences in their families' finances, do you think their upbringing under those circumstances would help or hinder them when trying to understand each other? Why?

9. Church is very important to Dawn. She sees it as her home-away-from-home. However, by viewing Tim as an outsider, is she overlooking the basic message of her faith? What is more important—going to church regularly or going for the right reasons? Is there anyone who does *not* belong in church?

10. Family dynamics are at work in everyone's life. Tim thinks he is going along with his family traditions for his mother's sake until he begins to relate to a little boy. Has the enthusiasm and blind trust of a child ever reminded you of what is really important in life? Have you acted on those thoughts? Are you glad you did?

*Melissa Hamilton returns to Davis Landing
with a growing secret in
PRODIGAL DAUGHTER, by Patricia Davids,
coming out in November 2006, only from
Steeple Hill Love Inspired.
Please turn the page for a sneak peek.*

Richard tucked his cell phone back in his pocket. The line of traffic hadn't moved, but at least the other lane was clear. He checked in his rearview mirror before pulling out and stopped short. Was that Melissa Hamilton leaving the bus station?

Turning his head to get a better view, he saw that he was right. She walked past him to the street corner. There, she set down her black duffel bag and raised a hand to sweep her long blond hair back over her shoulder.

She certainly was as lovely as ever. The overcast sky couldn't dim the taffy and honey brightness of her thick hair. It flowed in rippling waves almost to the center of her back. She was dressed in a flared skirt with big yellow sunflowers on a red background and a yellow blouse with short puff sleeves. Over her arms she had draped a red shawl with yellow fringe. Pulling the flimsy shawl up to cover her shoulders, she shivered and turned her back to the wind. The late October air definitely had a chill in it. As he watched her, the rain began in earnest. She glanced up, then lifted her shawl to cover her head.

Richard frowned. What on earth was the daughter of Wallace Hamilton doing coming into town on the bus?

Not that it mattered how she got here. The important thing was that she was home again. Wallace and Nora had both been worried sick about their youngest child. Melissa had left town with her boyfriend months ago and no one had heard from her since. That in itself was bad enough, but to disappear when her father was seriously ill seemed totally selfish. As the baby of the Hamilton family, she had always been overindulged and spoiled, but this time she had gone too far.

Wallace's publishing firm, Hamilton Media, was one of Richard's most important clients, but more than that, Wallace and Nora were his friends. He knew what a strain Wallace's leukemia and bone marrow transplant had put on the man and his family. That Melissa had run off without a word hadn't sat well with Richard and a lot of other people.

He had always hoped the loveable but wayward girl would come around and grow up into a responsible adult like the rest of the Hamilton kids, but maybe he had been wrong about her.

He watched as she tried to hail a cab, but the taxis in line already had fares. She looked around as if she didn't know what to do next. Suddenly, he was struck by how fragile and bewildered she looked.

Vivacious and flirty was the way he would have described Melissa five months ago. She had always used her charm, including batting those big brown eyes at men, in order to get her way. Now, the woman shivering on the corner simply looked tired and lost.

It only took him a moment to decide what to do next. It wasn't the first time he'd helped Melissa Hamilton out of a jam and it wasn't like to be the last. He pulled out around the taxis and stopped at the corner in front of her. He pressed the electric button and the passenger side window slid down. He leaned across the seat and called out, "Melissa, do you need a ride?"

Melissa jumped, startled by the sound of someone calling her name. She clutched her shawl more tightly and leaned down to look in the car that had pulled up beside her. Her father's attorney sat behind the wheel of a shiny, black sedan.

Melissa had to admit that Richard McNeil looked decidedly handsome in his charcoal-gray tailored suit and white button-down dress shirt minus a tie. It had always amazed her how such a big man could wear his clothes so well. With his rugged good looks, black hair and fabulous bright blue eyes, it wasn't surprising that she had suffered a crush on him in her teenage years. Maybe she still harbored a trace of it, she thought, if she were being honest with herself.

Of all the people who knew her family, why did

Richard McNeil have to be the one to see her slinking back into town?

"Mr. McNeil, what are you doing here?"

"It looks like I'm offering you a lift."

She hesitated, not sure what to do next. Glancing around, she saw that no empty taxi had appeared. Waiting for one would only prolong the inevitable encounter with her sister. She took a step toward the car. "I'd hate to be any trouble."

"It's no trouble. I'm on my way back to my office, but I can drop you off at your home if you like."

She bit her lip and hesitated, then said, "Could you drop me off at my sister Amy's instead?"

"Sure thing. Hop in before you get any wetter." A flurry of raindrops accompanied his words.

"All right. If you're sure it isn't any trouble." She picked up her bag, opened the door and slid into the front seat. Instantly, she was engulfed by the masculine scent of his aftershave, the smell of leather upholstery and the aroma of…was that pecan pie? Her stomach did a flip-flop.

"I put your bag in the trunk," he offered.

"No, this is fine. Thank you." She wrapped her arms around her duffel and held it tightly in her lap, hoping to hide her pregnancy for a little while longer. At five months she wasn't showing much, but it wouldn't be long before even her full skirt and baggy peasant blouse couldn't conceal how far Wallace Hamilton's youngest daughter had fallen.

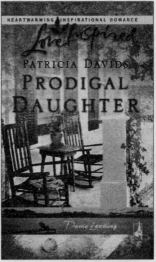

PRODIGAL DAUGHTER

Davis Landing

BY
PATRICIA DAVIDS

**Nothing is stronger
than a family's love.**

Single, pregnant and too
ashamed to face her family,
Melissa Hamilton turned to
family friend Richard McNeil.
He'd always been there for
her, and this was no exception.
Has this prodigal daughter
finally found her way home?

*Available November 2006
wherever you buy books.*

Steeple
Hill®

www.SteepleHill.com

LIPD

Love Inspired®

TITLES AVAILABLE NEXT MONTH

Don't miss these four stories in November

AT HOME IN DRY CREEK by Janet Tronstad
Dry Creek

With two kids to raise, and her ex-husband in jail, Barbara Strong moved to Dry Creek for a fresh start. Sheriff Carl Wall asked everyone—especially single cowboys—to leave Barbara alone so she could heal, though the Montana lawman hadn't anticipated breaking his own rule by falling for her.

PRODIGAL DAUGHTER by Patricia Davids
Davis Landing

Single and pregnant, Melissa Hamilton was reluctant to return home to her family, so she turned to Richard McNeil, the man who'd always been there for her. Richard wanted to protect Melissa from the cares of the world—would he ever see her as the woman she'd become?

WITH CHRISTMAS IN HIS HEART by Gail Gaymer Martin

Caring for her grandmother was a labor of love, but executive Christine Powers worried about the paper piling up in her office. Enter Will Lambert, her grandmother's enigmatic boarder. His laid-back style grew on her—and so did he—but Christine was facing a difficult choice: her heart or her career.

A HICKORY RIDGE CHRISTMAS by Dana Corbit

Five years ago, Hannah Woods had given birth as a teenager. She adored her little girl, but she'd never told Todd McBride he was a father. Todd had left town a boy and returned a man with a quest: to ask Hannah for a second chance. Yet Hannah's secret threw him into a tailspin.

LICNM1006